LOVE ME
good

Love Me Good: Citrus Pines Book 4
Copyright 2022 © Lila Dawes
The author asserts the moral right to be identified as the owner of this work.
No part of this book may be reproduced or transmitted in any form or by any means, including but not limited to: graphic, electronic, or mechanical, including photocopying, recording, taping, or by any informational storage retrieval system without advanced prior permission in writing from the publisher.

This is a work of fiction, and is not based on a true story or on real characters.

Cover image: Depositphotos.
Cover design: Lila Dawes.

Dedication

For all the good girls who wanted to rebel but never really knew how…

…this one is for you.

Authors Note

This novella contains the "hidden / secret identity" trope which means there will be some instances of deception.

This is the 4th book in the series and can be read as a standalone however there are some plot points mentioned which have been resolved in the previous book in the series, which is why, although mentioned, they are not a key focus in this story.

This novella contains mentions of the death of a character (villain in previous book), deception, multiple steamy descriptive sexual scenes, and familial conflict.

Love Me Good

Contents

Dedication	iii
Authors Note	iv
Contents	v
Chapter 1	7
Chapter 2	19
Chapter 3	26
Chapter 4	38
Chapter 5	47
Chapter 6	55
Chapter 7	61
Chapter 8	72
Chapter 9	81
Chapter 10	90
Chapter 11	103
Chapter 12	116
Chapter 13	128
Chapter 14	136
Chapter 15	143
Chapter 16	152
Chapter 17	162
Other Books By Lila Dawes	175
Acknowledgements	176

About the Author 177

Chapter 1

Aaaand you're a stalker.

An absolutely psychopathic stalker and you should be ashamed of yourself.

Who the hell moves across the country to be close to someone they've never met?

"This guy, that's who," Ben Morgan mumbled, gripping the door handle to the rustic bar in the small town of Citrus Pines. He took a deep breath, mulling over in his mind his completely ridiculous decision to uproot his entire life for someone he'd never met. Well, not in person anyway.

Would he recognize her right away? Would she be as amazing in person as she was online? Would he feel like shit when he met her boss that she was so freaking *obsessed* with? Ben hoped like hell that his resting bastard face didn't show when he met Taylor for their interview, that he could get through it politely and not scream *you sir, stole my girl!* His stomach flipped as he realized he was about to come face to face with his competition for her affection. He released his death-grip on the handle and turned back to pace along the porch of The Rusty Bucket Inn.

What the hell were you thinking? Coming to a new town, trying to get a job in the bar where she works? You'll be arrested within minutes. You can't even pretend you don't know her, the evidence is all over your computer...

He raked a hand through his dirty blond hair that had grown far too long. He didn't think he was a psychopath, that may be open to discussion right now, but he had found a deep connection with someone and he couldn't just ignore it. The only problem was, she lived halfway across the country and didn't even know what he looked like, what his real name was, or that he had changed his whole life to meet her.

Ben had met Kayleigh in a forum for a group role playing game they were part of. They had been commenting on the same thread and while drama kicked off between the other players, he messaged Kayleigh separately to continue a more level-headed discussion. Her knowledge and the constructive way she illustrated her point, not to mention her strategic thinking, had drawn him in and after they had won the game based on their teamwork, they kept chatting.

Now he logged on every day just to speak to her and it was the highlight of his day. They talked about their lives, their work and unfortunately about Kayleigh's crush on her boss. Every time she talked about Taylor's adorable red curls, piercings and tattoos, Ben died a little inside. Ben didn't have red hair, curly or straight. He didn't have tattoos or piercings. Taylor was probably six foot a million and stacked with muscle. Ben wasn't exactly short, but he didn't quite hit the magical six feet mark. And muscles? Psh, what muscles? He was Captain Lean.

He also didn't own his own business. In fact, he was a total failure.

He flunked out of med school, recently embarrassed his entire family at their annual end-of-summer cookout, before he hammered the final nail in the *disappointed parents* coffin when he abandoned his paramedic training. Following this absolute clusterfuck, he fled to Citrus Pines to be near the one person who understood him. The one person who never made him feel like a disappointment.

The way Kayleigh described the small town, it sounded charming, wholesome and accepting. He needed that after the last few years of pressure, anxiety and continual failure. He needed breathing space. He hadn't moved here *just* for Kayleigh, he wanted to get away from the hustle and bustle of the big city. Live a life away from overwhelming expectations of a career he had no interest in. He also liked the idea of connecting with people more and being able to greet his neighbors every morning without them glaring at him suspiciously like people in the city did.

He hadn't told Kayleigh what he'd done. She had no idea he'd packed up his life and moved. He didn't want to scare her. He just wanted to spend time with her and see if she would accept him in real life the way she did online. Then he would break the news to her that he was GreenEyedKing96, and she would be horrified and never speak to him again. Yeah, then again maybe not. Maybe he shouldn't tell her. Maybe he would just slowly start appearing online less and she would forget about

GreenEyedKing96 and focus on real life Ben? No, that also didn't feel right.

Either way, he was nearly late for his interview, and he needed to get his ass inside before he disappointed his potential new boss. He couldn't handle letting anyone else down right now.

He took a deep breath but before he reached for the door, it swung open, rebounding off the building with a *bang* and a man burst out. Ben glimpsed him for only a moment as the guy headed for the line of trees to the left of the bar, but Ben had time to spot the blood pouring from the guy's nose. *What the fuck?*

"Help! I need some help in here!" A woman shouted. Ben ran inside the bar, the burst of adrenaline giving him that unparalleled high he loved so much. Once inside he glanced around the empty bar but couldn't see a single soul. He headed towards the open door on the right and found a red-headed woman bent over another woman slumped on the floor.

"Oh my God, what happened?" His eyes took in the woman on the floor with blood coming from a wound on her head.

It's her.

It's Kayleigh.

He froze for a moment, gazing at the wonderful human that he'd been talking to for two years, finally in the flesh. Except right now, she was wounded. Her round cherub cheeks were pale, her light brown hair in disarray around her and her soft pink mouth pinched in pain.

"I need some ice, now!" The redhead snapped, jolting him back to the moment, and he ran off in search of ice. He headed down the corridor, found a door to the restrooms on one side and the kitchen on the other. He barged into the kitchen, his emergency responder-mode kicking in. He grabbed a metal bowl from the counter, shoved it under the faucet and filled it with cool water. While he waited for it to fill, he pulled out his cell phone and called for an ambulance. When they confirmed they were on their way, he switched off the stoves that were currently burning and locked the back door to the bar so no one could come in. He didn't know what had happened, but it had to be something to do with the guy who had ran outside, and Ben didn't want him sneaking in the back door. He grabbed some ice from the freezer and dumped it into the bowl, snagging a cloth and an empty bucket on his way back to the women.

"I've called an ambulance, locked up the back and turned off the stoves. We need to get her to stay awake. Keep talking to her until the ambulance arrives. And she's probably concussed so hold this bucket in case she needs to be sick," he said, trying to keep his voice calm, like his training had taught him. But it was tough not to panic when the injured party was someone you cared about. Ben dipped the cloth in the bowl and began gently dabbing at Kayleigh's brow and cheeks, her delicate skin turning pearlescent under the water droplets trickling down.

"Ka- uh, what's her name?" he asked, nearly revealing that he already knew exactly who this was.

"Kayleigh," the redhead replied.

"Kayleigh? Pretty. Okay Kayleigh you need to wake up now," he said, pulling Kayleigh back against his chest, resting her there. He noticed how tiny she seemed in his arms, so delicate.

"Who are you?" the redhead asked.

"I'm Ben Morgan. I'm here for my interview," he said, meeting her gaze. She was a stunning woman, long red curls, green eyes a shade darker than his own. He turned back to Kayleigh and continued to dab her face. He talked to her, random words coming out of his mouth about the weather and asking what her favorite type of dog was, even though he already knew she loved Saint Bernards. He just needed to try and keep her awake. And keep his own panic at bay. *Come on Ben, stay calm and just remember: be more E.P!*

Kayleigh stirred a little, her eyes fluttering open, and he got a glimpse of them up close. Startling blue-gray in color, like wild seas on a stormy day. His heart kicked in his chest as he fell a little bit deeper in love with her.

How can you love someone you've never met?

"Taylor?" Kayleigh groaned. Ben's stomach dipped. He'd forgotten all about his competition. *Of course she's asking for Taylor, she's in love with the guy!*

"I'm here Kayleigh," the redhead replied, taking Kayleigh's hand.

Ben frowned, then his eyebrows lifted as realization settled in. Taylor was a *woman*? He'd thought that Taylor was this sexy buff guy with… red hair in adorable curls… tattoos and piercings… Ben ran his eyes over the woman next to him and everything clicked.

Kayleigh had never said that Taylor was a man, he'd just *assumed* that. Then another thought slid into place: not only was she not in love with Ben, he'd assumed Kayleigh was straight, but the evidence that that wasn't the case was sitting right next to him. Now he knew, Kayleigh would never be his. Another lump filled his throat. *This is why you don't do stupid things, like move hundreds of miles for a woman you've never met and clearly didn't know as well as you thought.* His romantic dreams of walking into the sunset hand in hand with Kayleigh crumbled to dust, the disappointment choking him.

Kayleigh groaned again in his arms and Ben cleared his

throat. "I'm not a doctor but I think she's concussed."

Kayleigh's eyes fluttered open again and she sighed, beaming at Taylor. "I love you!"

The phantom knife currently protruding from Ben's heart twisted sharply.

"Aw, I love you too, Kay," Taylor patted her hand affectionately, but Kayleigh moaned.

"No, you beautiful dummy. I *love* you," Kayleigh said again.

Taylor's eyes flicked to Ben, and he gave her a tight smile. He knew Kayleigh would be mortified if Taylor found out how in love with her she truly was. "Yeah, she doesn't know what she's saying, I'd ignore that," he said casually.

Taylor nodded and Ben turned his attention back to Kayleigh whose eyes were closing again.

Then the ambulance arrived, and two paramedics ran in, pushing Ben and Taylor to the side as they got to work checking Kayleigh's vital signs. Ben continued to hover, watching them work and checking that they did all the things he would have done, that they weren't skipping any steps. He turned away, reminding himself that he wasn't a fully qualified paramedic. He had walked out on his training, so he shouldn't be judging anyone right now.

"So, um shall we reschedule my interview. I'm free anytime?" Ben said, tucking his hands in the pockets of his jeans and trying to distract himself from what was happening with his most favorite person in the world. His stomach twisted; it was torture to see her like this.

Taylor turned to him. "Fuck your interview, you're hired. When can you start?"

His eyes flicked to Kayleigh, and he worried a hand over his stubbly jaw, suddenly doubting that this was the best idea he ever had. Maybe he needed to think about it, maybe he'd been too impulsive. He had made a rash decision and now he had information that he didn't have before.

"Really?"

Taylor nodded eagerly.

"I guess I can start next week?" he said. That way he could have a week to think about if he really wanted to do this. At least if he decided it wasn't the best thing for him then he hadn't wasted too much of her time.

"Perfect! Wait, how old are you?" she asked.

"I'm twenty-six and a non-smoking Sagittarius who likes long walks on the beach and quiet nights in," he quipped, then his smile fell as he mentally checked himself. "Ah, sorry about that, my mouth runs away with me sometimes."

Her grin quirked up. "Then we're gonna get along just fine. And with Kayleigh too, you're the same age so you'll probably have a lot in common."

He looked over at Kayleigh again, watching as the paramedics put her on a stretcher and concern gripped him tight. "Yeah, we probably do."

As Ben was deep in thought, two men rushed into the bar, one of them heading straight for Taylor and hugging her tightly. The other one, dressed all in black and sporting an extremely intense stare, ran suspicious eyes over Ben.

As Taylor explained what happened, Ben realized he'd come in at the end of the ordeal. If only he'd gone inside the bar sooner, he could have prevented Kayleigh from getting hurt. But no, he was busy having an existential crisis outside.

"Who are you?" Intense Stare Guy demanded. Ben was pretty tall and kinda on the lean side but this guy, in fact both of these men, were fucking huge.

Love Me Good

"I'm Ben Morgan, I'm new in town. I came here for an interview and saw a guy rushing out of the bar and then I heard someone calling for help and I came inside. I helped as best I could and called the ambulance."

"Are you prepared to give a witness statement?" he asked. Well, not really asked, more like growled his demand.

"Anything for my new boss," Ben smiled, trying to win over whoever this guy was.

"Right, let's head to the station then. I'll get a man posted in the area to keep an eye on the bar and your cabin, see if this asshole shows his face again," he told Taylor then ushered Ben out of the bar and gestured towards a vehicle which had *Citrus Pines Sheriff* scrawled along the side.

"Man, if I had to pick anyone to be sheriff of a town I was living in, it would be you any day of the week," Ben said. The sheriff frowned at him but said nothing and Ben cringed at his lack of a filter.

They drove in silence to the station which was a mercifully short distance. If it had been any longer, Ben would have begun trying to make awkward small talk to distract himself from the worry about Kayleigh. And neither of them wanted that. The sheriff got out of the car and stormed inside the station, leaving Ben to run after him.

Ben entered the small building and looked around, a wide grin splitting his lips. It was the epitome of a small-town sheriff's office and he felt like he'd walked onto a movie set. Dark wood décor was everywhere he looked, the hum of the air conditioner was the backing track to the main tune of phones ringing, keyboards clacking and the low murmur of conversation. The building was small, only a few desks inside with two offices, and an old staircase leading down to a basement.

"Any messages?" The sheriff spoke to an older man at one of the desks.

"Not in the ten minutes you've been gone," the old man replied with a good-natured grin, his white bushy eyebrows waggling.

The sheriff grunted. "Justine teaching you sass as well as Spanish?"

The old man burst out laughing. "I taught her everything she knows about sass. What time are you two coming round for dinner tomorrow night?"

Ben watched as the sheriff's face softened. "The usual time. Are we cooking the trout we caught last weekend?"

"You bet."

"Can't wait." The sheriff finally gestured to Ben. "This is Ben Morgan. He's here to give a statement on the call-out we just had, so hold any new calls until we're done." Then Ben was being dragged into an office and he noticed the name stenciled on the door read *Deputy Sheriff Blake Miller*.

Blake proceeded to interrogate him to a degree where Ben nearly requested his lawyer. *Nearly*. Because that would mean calling his father to ask who his lawyer actually was, and he was avoiding his family right now.

When Ben was declared free to go, he wandered around the town, stopping at Ruby's Diner for some food and again was struck by how retro it was. Like something out of a 1950s movie. *This town is perfect, exactly what I'm looking for right now.*

"Hey there, sweet cheeks. You look familiar, have we been intimately acquainted before?"

Ben turned towards the voice that sounded like someone had smoked fifty a day for their entire life. He came face to face with a woman who couldn't be younger than eighty and sported bright purple hair, electric blue glasses and smudged pink lipstick.

"I don't think so, ma'am," he replied, trying to fight off the shudder that mental image gave him.

"Hmm." She narrowed her eyes, not convinced. Ben got recognized every now and then, that was what happened when you had a famous father and your brother was slowly making a name for himself. *While you ran away like a big disappointment. Guess the ol' man was right about you.*

"So, what's a pretty little thing like you doing here?" The woman asked, wiping down the Formica counter.

Ben tugged at the collar of his shirt. "I'm not entirely sure myself."

"Well, why don't you have a slice of pie while you think it over. My name's Ruby and this is my diner," she said, cutting him a slice of cherry pie.

"I think I'll do just that."

"And if you're feeling a bit chatty then that's okay too."

"I'm Ben, nice to meet you, ma'am." He stuck out his hand and she stared at it before she shook it.

"That's a mighty fine grip you've got there, son. Maybe we *should* get intimately acquainted after all." Ruby winked at him. Although she was propositioning him, she did it with such charm that he couldn't help himself; he barked out a laugh.

"I think I'll just have the pie for now, Ruby. I'll let you know if I need anything else."

"You kind of remind me of someone… are you sure we haven't met before?"

"Oh, I think I would remember you," he replied, and she tittered at him, flashing him a coy smile.

He ate his pie, chatted with Ruby some more and

wondered whether it would be a red flag to call the hospital to find out about Kayleigh. Deciding that yes it probably would be, he went back to the motel where he was staying, feeling no clearer on the decision he'd made. Matt, his brother, would never doubt his decision, he would've made the right decision the first time, as would their father. But comparing himself to them did him no good, it just made him feel like shit.

He kicked off his shoes and went over to the closet and opened it. He stared at the outfit in front of him, the one that had simultaneously broken him and set him free. He trailed his fingers over the white satin, the ruby, orange, and black rhinestones glinting in the light. He had a yearning unlike any other to put it on, to feel that rush, but he pushed it down, shutting the closet door.

He turned to the cage in the corner of the room and stuck his fingers through the bar, tousling the long white fur of his pet rabbit.

"Did you miss me, Geralt?"

Geralt proceeded to lick his fingers then nibbled, because Geralt could be a dick sometimes. "Okay, I deserved that. You won't have to be in the cage long, it's just until we get our own place and then you'll be free again, I promise," he crooned at the beast and Geralt gave a sassy flick of his head. Ben added some more hay to the holder which Geralt proceeded to fling everywhere.

That night he sat alone in his motel room, spinning in his chair in front of the computer, talking to Geralt and waiting for the chime that signified Kayleigh was online. And when that tell-tale chime filled the room, a smile split his face and the breath he hadn't known he'd been holding released in a *whoosh*.

GoodGirlKay: Hey you :)

Chapter 2

GreenEyedKing96: Hey beautiful, how you doing? I missed you.

As soon as the message appeared, Kayleigh's horrible day disappeared and a smile slid across her lips for the first time. *Are you concerned that a total stranger has such power over your emotions? He's not a total stranger, I know he's a* he *at least!* Ugh, maybe she did need help. But if there was one person guaranteed to make her feel better right now, it was GreenEyedKing96.

She was home after a particularly challenging day: she had been attacked at the bar where she worked when Taylor's stalker ex-boyfriend turned up. He had gotten violent, shoved Kayleigh into a door and she cracked her head on it, getting a concussion. Then in her concussed state, she had accidentally declared her love for the aforementioned boss. *Then* she had spent all day at the hospital before her boss, the one she declared her love to, turned up to take her home. Taylor had brought Kayleigh home to her parents who completed the humiliation by fussing over her injuries. Her mother clucking like a hen, like Kayleigh wasn't a twenty-six-year-old woman. Now she was alone in her room and finally able to decompress, all she wanted to do was get into bed and never get out again.

Cheese and crackers, why did you tell Taylor you loved her? Kayleigh groaned out loud as she replayed the moment. She had loved Taylor since the moment she'd met the feisty redhead. She was so enamored with Taylor that half the time she could barely speak to her, too shy and too scared she would make a fool of herself, which she *always* did.

But her love for Taylor was destined to be unrequited because Taylor liked men. Technically, Kayleigh did too. She'd realized she was bisexual when she was a teenager but didn't have the courage to tell her parents. She still hadn't said those words aloud to them, but they knew. One day she was talking to her mom about her favorite actress, Jennifer Lawrence and obsessed a little too much. Her mom had stared at her like she could read her thoughts and Kayleigh's heart stopped. Then her mom said that Jennifer Lawrence was a beautiful woman and that it was perfectly okay if Kayleigh found women attractive.

Despite a couple of relationships with both men and women, Kayleigh had never really had that spark, that connection with someone. She figured it was because she was young and hadn't really *lived* yet. She didn't have much life experience at only twenty-six, but it was something that had been on her mind recently.

Love Me Good

Kayleigh had always been shy. She had never spoken up much in class at school, afraid she would say the wrong thing and embarrass herself. She didn't have much confidence and never felt like she fit in. When she realized she was bisexual, she felt like that made her stand out even more in such a small town. Combined with generic awkward teenage angst, it pushed her confidence further down.

She'd just wanted to hide away and not face the real world, and that's how she found the online gaming community. Kayleigh found her place to shine and made friends with like-minded people who understood her. She finally felt accepted. Anyone who said online friends weren't real friends just didn't get it. The gaming community was her happy place. The place to go to talk about her passion and connect with people who shared that passion. She built her confidence, her social skills and discovered her dream.

She wanted to be a narrative designer for games. To be the one to create the story and the game mechanics behind it. Only she didn't have the confidence to go for what she wanted. It was her dream but what if no one liked her writing? What if she couldn't do it? What if she failed? She was just Kayleigh Good from Citrus Pines, a minuscule town in the middle of nowhere. What could she ever achieve?

GreenEyedKing96: You there, Kay?

The chime from his message brought her out of her thoughts. Someone she did have a connection with was GreenEyedKing96. He intrigued her. She was curious to know what he looked like, not that looks were that important to her, but it would help to build her impression of him. She knew he didn't have a great relationship with his family. Sometimes when he told her the things his father or brother said, she just wanted to hug him and tell him everything would be okay, that one day what they thought wouldn't matter. But she had to settle for typing to him instead. He was her best friend, yet she'd never even met him. She hated that he was so far away, so many times she had begged him to move here but it looked like it wasn't meant to be.

If she could meet someone and have the connection with them that she had with GreenEyedKing96 then she would die a happy woman. He was funny, caring and so sweet. They had a lot in common and he didn't want her to be someone she wasn't. He accepted her, no questions asked. She shared her love of writing stories for games and even trusted him enough to let him read the fanfiction she'd written about the game they played, after a huge amount of cajoling on his part.

They had developed a beautiful friendship, but she would be lying if she said she didn't want something more. Was it weird to feel a sexual connection with someone when you hadn't met them, and nothing more than light flirting happened with them? She wasn't afraid to admit that a few times after a deep conversation with him and some *extremely* mild flirting that she had put out the lights, lit her scented candles and had some alone time with her vibrator, picturing his face.

All she knew about him physically was that he had green eyes. The speculation over which shade of green had kept her awake some nights. Maybe she should just ask him for a picture? *It would only be fair, he knows what you look like...* She had a picture of herself as her profile pic but his was an avatar. Most of the male gamers online had towering men, muscular beasts or buxom women as their avatars, but GreenEyedKing96? He had a fluffy white bunny and that just made Kayleigh like him even more.

She pulled herself closer to her computer, staring down at the lights flashing all over her keyboard, the internal fan whirring loudly, struggling to keep the masses of computer components cool. Her fingers flew as she typed out her embarrassment.

GoodGirlKay: Yeah, just had a nightmare day and could use my friend :) Got hurt at work, confessed my love to my boss and this was in front of the new guy who looked after me until the ambulance came. I can't even remember his face but I bet he'll remember mine. #sob.

GreenEyedKing96: You got hurt? Are you okay?

GoodGirlKay: I'm fine. Just a concussion and stitches are sexy, right? Anyway, it's a long story.

GreenEyedKing96: Declared your love to your boss? #Awks.

GoodGirlKay: For sure! Now I need to quit, get a new identity, leave town and never come back.

GreenEyedKing96: No way, you can't quit now!

GoodGirlKay: Why not, it's just a bar job?

GreenEyedKing96: Just because. You're not a quitter Kay, I believe in you.

GoodGirlKay: Anyway, moving on from my humiliation… how did your job interview go?

GreenEyedKing96: Really well, I got offered the job.

GoodGirlKay: Yaaaay congrats!! Tell me you took it?

GreenEyedKing96: I'm mulling things over… I would start in a week so haven't got long to decide.

GoodGirlKay: Take. The. Darn. Job.

GreenEyedKing96: Yes ma'am, lol.

GoodGirlKay: I know you're worried about what your family thinks after the whole 'abandoning your medical career thing' but you have to think about yourself and what you want. So, what do you want?

GreenEyedKing96: Very good point. I think I want that job.

GoodGirlKay: That was easy haha! You're very susceptible to persuasion.

GreenEyedKing96: Well, you're very persuasive...

She giggled as his message popped onto the screen and felt her cheeks flush, her pulse skittering as she pictured those green eyes, *what shade dammit,* glittering enticingly on the other side of his computer screen. She wanted to take it further and flirt but didn't know what to say, she was too out of practice.

She needed confidence; she knew she did. She just didn't know how to get it. She was too self-aware and self-conscious. Lack of confidence was embedded in her DNA and she didn't know how to change it. So, until she figured out what to do, she would continue being boring computer geek, plain Kayleigh.

She and GreenEyedKing96 chatted some more but no more flirting happened. And when she went to bed, she lit her scented candles and then gave in to her fantasies of him coming to her hometown to rescue her.

*

The next morning she woke up feeling flat. Taylor had said to take as much time as she needed before coming back to work, which was just as well because Kayleigh didn't feel like doing *anything*. Except wallowing. Wallowing felt pretty good.

So that was what she did all week. She ignored her life, ignored her gaming and she even ignored

GreenEyedKing96. Her parents kept checking on her, obviously concerned, but she didn't know what to tell them.

Kayleigh didn't even know what was wrong.

*

Chapter 3

When the week was up Kayleigh finally came out of hibernation. She had spent too long wallowing and if she was honest, she wasn't sure her week of staying in bed had made her feel any better. It was too stuffy in her room, her head was pounding and she needed air. She needed to leave her room. She needed to see people and get back to life.

That morning she got on her bicycle and rode to work, stopping briefly to pick up Mr. Henderson's morning paper. When she handed it to him over the fence, he complained that she was a few minutes later than normal and the morning dew had ruined the sports section. Kayleigh swallowed her retort and continued on her way before stopping to take Mrs. Steinman's dog out. Mrs. Steinman, instead of thanking her, shouted that she better

Love Me Good

make sure Misty went number one *and* number two because last time Kayleigh didn't check and Misty number two'd all over her nice new carpet. Kayleigh offered Mrs. Steinman her polite smile and got back on her bicycle before she screamed *take your own dang dog out in future!*

Then she had to swerve around the Carsons' two children who were roughhousing and spilled into Kayleigh's path. She fell off her bike, skinning her knee, but they took no notice. She bit her lip to stop from cussing at them; they were only young and didn't deserve it.

By the time The Rusty Bucket Inn came into view, Kayleigh was beginning to feel as though she should have continued hibernating.

People sucked. They took advantage and were never grateful and Kayleigh was too much of a coward to ever say what was on her mind. She locked up her bike and trudged into the bar, her knee throbbing and stinging like a son of a gun.

She paused before opening the door to the bar. She was not looking forward to facing Taylor after she had stupidly declared her love. Collecting herself, she went inside but instead of the beautiful redhead she was expecting, there was a strange man behind the bar. Dirty blond hair that was long and tousled in that *I just got out of bed* way that was so popular with men these days. Medium height and build with trim waist and hips. His black T-shirt clung to his back as he wiped down the bar surface and she spotted toned biceps flexing away.

"Um…hello?" she called. The guy spun around, his eyes running up and down her form before he released a breath. He wiped a hand over his mouth and his expression blanked.

"Hi, Kayleigh, right?" he asked. His deep baritone was

smooth, like cool Irish cream.

"Yeah. Who're you?"

"I'm Ben, the newbie," he said, then propped his hip against the bar, folding his arms over his chest and raising one side of his mouth in a smirk. He crossed his ankles, and her eyes were drawn to his dark blue jeans, turned up at the ankles displaying shiny black boots. She swallowed thickly at the way he looked so effortlessly cool, like he owned the place, and annoyance flitted through her at how seamlessly he fit in when she never felt like she had.

Then she realized this was the guy who had helped her when Taylor's ex, Dale, had shoved her into the door in his bid to escape. She knew she should be grateful for Ben's assistance, and she definitely was, but she was also mortified that he had seen her at one of her worst moments.

"Uh, nice to meet you. Thanks for your help the other day," she mumbled, staring at her feet as the heat in her cheeks grew.

"No sweat," he replied, and she spotted his casual shrug out the corner of her eye. She flicked her gaze up, running over him. She'd never seen him before, and she prided herself on knowing most of the locals. *He must be from out of town.* She definitely would have remembered that blond hair and those breathtaking pale green eyes that reminded her of mint chocolate chip ice cream. GreenEyedKing96 popped into her head just then, were his the same shade? His stupid lean body that made her want to strip off his clothes and see what delights lay underneath. Ben's smirk deepened like he could read her thoughts and she abruptly headed towards Taylor's office to store her bike helmet.

"Oh my baby girl, I'm so glad you're here!" Taylor gasped and then Kayleigh was enveloped in her arms, inhaling Taylor's wonderful scent that made her pulse pound, and she tightened her hold. When Taylor stepped back, she cupped Kayleigh's cheeks but Kayleigh shrugged her off, worried her *I love you* was screaming from her eyes, humiliation crushing her again.

"Yep, I'm back. So, we have a new guy?" She tried to seem unaffected and disinterested but her words just sounded hollow.

"Yes! Ben seems like he'll be a great fit around here and I bet you two will have lots in common. He's new to town so maybe you could show him around?" Taylor had that gleam in her eye that Kayleigh loved so much, except when she realized Taylor was hinting at a potential romance between her and Ben. "I'm sure he'd really appreciate that," Taylor added, sitting herself back behind her desk.

"Doubtful," Kayleigh muttered under her breath. Taylor frowned and Kayleigh mentally kicked herself for letting her despondent mood turn her catty.

"Also, he hasn't worked in a bar before so he'll pretty much need showing how to do everything."

"Anything else?" Kayleigh asked, trying to stop another catty response from leaving her lips.

"I missed you." Taylor smiled sweetly and Kayleigh's insides twisted.

"Missed you too," she replied, swallowing around the lump in her throat. *Like you wouldn't believe.*

With a wave, Kayleigh went back out to the bar and found Ben looking back and forth between the bottles of whiskey and brandy in his hands, his blond brow furrowed quizzically as he consulted the cocktail menu in front of him.

"Confused about which alcohol is which?"

Her words caused him to jolt and he nearly dropped

the bottles. She took them from him and placed them back on the bar before turning to face him. He frowned down at her, then quickly turned his attention to an attractive woman who sidled up to the bar. Although Kayleigh couldn't blame him—the woman was stunning—hurt that she had no right to be feeling pricked at her and her stomach sank. *He's just another man who is more interested in a prettier face.*

She spent the next few hours showing Ben how to pour pints, mix cocktails and change a keg over. Several times she tried to engage him in conversation, but his responses were minimal. *How on earth did Taylor think we would have lots in common?*

Taylor was buzzing around them nonstop, like she couldn't wait for the shift to be over. "Okay guys, thanks for tonight but you can take off now, I wanna close up!" She whirled around them, all frantic excitement.

"But it's still ten minutes to closing," Kayleigh pointed out, confusion pinching her forehead.

"I know but I'm eager to go and there's no one here, so take some time back and skedaddle!" Taylor circled around them both and pushed them towards the door.

"I need my helmet." Kayleigh scampered into the office and retrieved said helmet, grimacing when she realized it was her really old one that had a Barbie sticker on the front.

Taylor practically shoved her and Ben out the door. Once outside, Ben turned to face her and then laughed when he looked at her helmet.

He tapped the Barbie sticker. "Real cute," he snorted.

Her pride stung and she grabbed her bike and swung her leg over. "See you tomorrow," she called out, hating how her voice wobbled, and pedaled away as fast as she could.

Love Me Good

She thought she heard him shout something after her but she kept going, worried the tears she'd been holding back all day would escape. The breeze tickled her stinging knee and she looked down, taking in her tatty jean shorts, dirty white sneakers and boring white tank top. *No wonder he isn't impressed by you. No one is.*

When Kayleigh made it home, she went straight to her room and got into bed, her mood the lowest it had been since the incident at the bar. As she lay under her blanket, her brain went to town on her, mocking her life choices, destroying her thoughts and her very last drop of confidence. She was twenty-six and what was she doing with life? Nothing. She never did anything exciting. Never did anything crazy or stood out. She didn't dare, her lack of confidence crippled her from doing anything exhilarating. From *living*.

She wasn't setting the world on fire; she was letting her fear overrule her: Fear of speaking up and confirming who she was, fear of becoming the person she truly wanted to be. She was constantly afraid people would laugh or tell her she couldn't do it, that her dreams were too big for a small-town girl.

But did Taylor care if she drew attention? Hell no, it was one of the reasons Kayleigh was so enamored with her. Maybe she needed a motto, like 'be more Taylor'? Or an alter ego? Like how Beyoncé had Sasha Fierce. *Kayleigh 2.0.* She mulled it over in her mind. Either way, she needed to change. Now. Or her soul would wither under the weight of her inability to choose happiness for herself. She was going to do what she wanted, when she wanted, how she damn well wanted.

Urgency consumed her. An impulse to burn the world to the ground and arise from the ashes reborn tore across her spirit, firing her senses. Obviously, she couldn't do that, but this energy needed to go somewhere.

She glanced around her room looking for a way to release this force. Her eyes caught on the scissors in her stationery holder and she leapt for them. She ran to the mirror on her dressing table and shoved herself down onto the chair, staring at herself. Her eyes wide, *wild*, with hope and excitement. Before she could change her mind, she grabbed a fistful of her mousey brown hair. She hacked away at it, feeling more rebellious by the second. Exhilaration burned bright inside her as her long locks floated down around her.

She laughed, a harsh choked sound, as she realized she had been her own oppressor. Then she looked at herself in the mirror as she cut in some bangs. *Bangs*! She was always told her face was too round for bangs, but Kayleigh 2.0 didn't care if her round face clashed with her choppy, edgy bangs. She was doing what *she* wanted.

Seconds later she was on her feet and running downstairs. Grabbing her purse and cycle helmet she headed for the door.

"Kayleigh, darling, are you going out?" her mother called.

Kayleigh paused, her mouth opened ready to assure her mother of exactly where she was going and when she would be back.

Just like she normally would.

Just like a good girl.

But Kayleigh 2.0 faltered. "Yep."

"Where are you going?" Her mom, Maureen, appeared around the door frame, dish towel in hand.

Kayleigh shrugged. "Out."

"Well, when are you back?"

"I dunno, later."

"Oh my gosh, what happened to your hair?" Maureen

gasped.

Kayleigh shrugged again, trying to shake off the fear of her mom's disapproval. "I changed it."

"Darling, is everything okay?"

"No, but it will be." Kayleigh smiled wide then left the house, slamming the front door in her haste. She leapt onto her bike and pedaled as fast as her legs would go to the late-night pharmacy the next town over. When the bright lights came into view, she hopped off her bike, not even bothering to hook it up to the bike rack, just leaving it on the sidewalk.

She hurried inside the old building, scouring the shelves for hair dye.

"No, no, no!" she groaned, rummaging through the boring natural colors, the gray coverage and root touch up.

Didn't the world understand she wanted *vibrance*?

She *deserved* it.

Kayleigh rounded the aisle and found exactly what she was looking for. Grabbing the shade *Awkward Peach* she headed for the register but stopped when she passed a mini make-up concession. It held only a few shades and the basics: mascara, eyeliner, and so on, but she was drawn to the dark lipsticks. Time for a complete change.

A few minutes later she made her way to the register with her hands full and covered in tester lines of lipstick in every shade, her skin striped with indecision. The clerk looked at her and raised an eyebrow, taking in her choppy haircut, flushed cheeks and wild eyes.

"Just put it all on my credit card."

She ran out of the pharmacy, so thrilled with her purchases and eager to get home and experiment that she nearly missed it. Her eyes caught the notice board, full of local advertisements and business cards. But there was a bright pink leaflet pinned with a graphic of a female silhouette in heels, leaning against a pole.

Kayleigh's blood pounded in her ears. It was a sign, she was sure. She had always been intrigued by pole dancing, found it fascinating to watch the way bodies contorted and moved and the strength the women had. She yearned to do something like that, something where she could let go, gain confidence and maybe even feel sexy?

She'd never felt sexy in her life but maybe it was time she started.

*

The next morning Kayleigh cycled to the bar. She didn't stop to pick up Mr. Henderson's paper. She didn't offer to take Mrs. Steinman's dog out for a number one or two and she dinged her bell repeatedly when approaching the Carsons' two little menaces until they flew out of her way. Kayleigh 2.0 wasn't rude but she no longer went out of her way to help others when their only response was to berate her.

Waving at Ruby as she opened up the diner, Kayleigh adjusted her helmet, *sans* Barbie sticker. Just because Kayleigh 2.0 was a badass didn't mean she couldn't be safety conscious.

She made it to the bar and took a deep breath as she secured her bike to the porch, then stilled herself to go inside. Would Taylor notice she had colored her hair? Would she notice her sultry make up that YouTube tutorials had taught her to apply? Did it matter if she did? *Taylor is straight and you need to get that through your thick skull, lady!* She needed to get over this crush, lust, love, whatever it was before she humiliated herself even more.

Love Me Good

Kayleigh 2.0 demanded it.

She shoved her thoughts away, loosening her shoulders and pushing open the door to The Rusty Bucket Inn. The familiar scent of stale alcohol and husky rock star voice blaring from the jukebox had her instantly feeling like she was home. She stopped in front of Taylor's office door, eyeing it suspiciously, still wary after the incident, like it might leap out and attack her.

Ben appeared carrying a case of beer, his arms flexed tightly against the weight. Today he had his hair slicked back, his T-shirt white instead of black.

"'Sup" she called, placing her hand on her hip and popping it out to the side, trying to project some sass. She'd decided Kayleigh 2.0 was gonna be sassy.

Ben's eyes widened before he blinked rapidly. Even from where she was standing, she couldn't miss those eyes of his. Soft green, like jade. The dynamic color startled her new cool girl persona and she smiled softly, losing her aloofness.

"Uh...did you change your hair since yesterday?" His eyes scanned her hair then down over her pushed up breasts, which were looking fabulous if she did say so herself, before sliding over the curve of her hips and resting on her thighs, highlighted by the black lace dress she'd hacked off at mid-thigh this morning.

"Yeah, I guess," she shrugged, like she was bored. Exactly how he had done to her.

"Looks..." He paused and his mouth flapped a bit like he was trying to find the words. Her stomach plummeted. "...great?"

She squinted at him. "Are you asking me if it looks great or telling me?"

"Telling you?" His velvet-laced voice squeaked a bit at the end, but shivers still danced down her spine. Why did the thought of him not liking her new look make her want to curl up into a ball and hide?

Before she could answer, he spun away and began wiping down the back bar. The muscles in his forearms tensing with each stroke had her mouth running dry. He was a hard worker, she would give him that. Yesterday, he had done everything she asked him to do and today he had started without her instead of waiting to be given something to do. Maybe she had been too harsh on him yesterday.

"Thanks again for looking after me last week. I feel like if you hadn't been here, things would have been a whole lot worse."

He shrugged again in that cool guy way, a lazy lift of one shoulder. Her eyes became transfixed on his broad hands, long tapered fingers, thick veins raised and coursing through the tan skin as he began to dry a glass. She was so drawn to them she barely heard his response.

"All part of the job," he grunted.

"The job?"

"Uh… I've had first aid training before, so I knew what to do," he said, coughing discreetly. His expression became sheepish, his cheeks adorably pink and she decided there and then that he was one of the best-looking men she'd ever seen.

"Well, thanks again," she said, smiling at him. She spotted his eyes lock onto her dimples, her stupid dimples that made her look like a child.

He frowned deeply and grunted, "Don't mention it," before turning away. Like he was used to women swooning over his lovely green eyes and attractive forearms. She didn't miss the way he looked her up and down before his eyes flitted away, dismissing her with a confidence she hadn't seen on someone other than

Love Me Good

Taylor.
It's time to change that, Kayleigh 2.0 reminded her.

*

Chapter 4

"I would like to return the favor. You're new in town, right? I could, like, show you around? Or not, I mean, whatever. I don't even like this town, so…" Her sweet voice trailed off and Ben turned back to face her. Her words replayed in his ears. *Really? The Kayleigh I know online loves* this town. *So much so that she even made me want to live here.*

His eyes took in her peach hair in choppy waves down to her shoulders, the new bangs framing her oval cheeks that made her look even more adorable. Her dark red-slicked mouth was playing havoc with his insides. Did she know how many times in the last few minutes he'd thought about sliding his tongue across those harlot lips to see if she tasted as sinful as she looked?

She appeared different from yesterday. She wasn't the

soft, gentle woman he knew. She was hard, snarky and a little edgier than he'd thought. He'd been so thrown off when he met her, awed by her that his silence and awkwardness had potentially come across like indifference. But now she matched his aloof behavior, maybe even liking it. Surely if she didn't, she wouldn't have made the offer hanging between them?

If she liked him indifferent, then indifferent he would be, if it meant he got to spend time with her. They hadn't had much chance to talk but he hoped that would change.

"I guess, maybe." He raised his shoulder again casually and let it drop. He bent down and began putting the beers in the fridge.

"Oh my God, what happened to you?" Kayleigh exclaimed.

Ben bolted upright at Kayleigh's shocked tone. Taylor had come out from her office. He had only greeted Taylor through the door this morning when he arrived, he hadn't actually seen her yet. Now he spotted her split lip, bruised cheek and bandaged fingers. She looked like she'd been through the wars, and Ben's stomach twisted at the sight, but the pain in Taylor's eyes was the saddest thing.

"Last night after you both left, Dale came back," Taylor said. From what Ben gathered when he was questioned last week, Dale was Taylor's ex-boyfriend who was stalking her and was the one who had attacked them when Kayleigh was injured in the crossfire.

"He wasn't happy about me and Beau's relationship and wanted to hurt Beau. Luckily, before anything really serious happened to us, Blake turned up. But Dale had a knife and wouldn't stop going after Beau, so Blake didn't have a choice, he…he shot him. Dale's dead," Taylor finished on a shuddering breath.

Kayleigh gasped, her hand covering her mouth and

she pulled Taylor into a tight hug. "Oh my God, that's awful! Are you okay? Where's Beau?" she asked, running her hands over Taylor's shaking arms.

"I think I'm still in shock, it hasn't sunk in yet. I feel sad about Dale but after everything he's done… I'm just glad it's all over now and no one else will get hurt. After all this time, I just want to get back to work and move on. And Beau, he's…" Taylor trailed off and avoided Kayleigh's eyes before biting her lip.

"He's okay?" Ben asked.

"Yeah, he's fine. But he's left, he needed some space after everything," Taylor replied miserably.

"He'll be back, he just needs time."

"I don't know if he will, Kayleigh."

"Then you need to have faith. Trust me," Kayleigh commanded.

Ben smiled as Kayleigh comforted Taylor. Seeing the two of them together reminded him how Kayleigh really felt about Taylor. That it didn't matter how he acted or how much time he spent with Kayleigh, she was never going to fall for him. He had to figure out whether he was okay just being her friend or if he would always want more. Staring at her now, the soft lighting in the bar glowing in her silky peach hair, bouncing off her stormy eyes, she ensnared him, there was no denying it.

Taylor turned to him. "How was your first night, not scared off after all that, are you?" she joked weakly, her heart not in it. Kayleigh turned and headed for Taylor's office where she stored the bike helmet that no longer sported the cute Barbie sticker he'd spotted yesterday. He watched her go, her black lace dress flouncing around the backs of her knees, teasing him. When had he found the backs of someone's knees sexy before? God, he needed help.

"Not at all. Looking forward to getting stuck in and working with you both," he replied.

Taylor smiled at him, but it didn't quite reach her eyes. "I'm glad."

Kayleigh was a little quiet for the rest of their shift, no doubt it was because she was worried about Taylor. At closing time she insisted on hanging around until Taylor was safely back in the cabin where she lived out back of the bar. When they watched Taylor close the door behind her, Kayleigh turned to Ben.

"See you tomorrow, I guess," she said, heading over to a bike tied to the porch.

"You want me to give you a ride home?" he asked, needing to spend more time with her.

"I don't think my bike will fit in your car."

"I can fold the seats down," he countered. She stared at him before shrugging again and he bit back a chuckle. She followed him wordlessly to his car and he folded down the back seats then proceeded to try and get her bike in the back. A lot of cursing and a few attempts later, his lateral brain had figured it out and finally the bike slotted in beautifully.

"I'm impressed," she quipped, and he saw the first genuine smile from her all night and was struck dumb at the sight of it.

"Well, I'm not just a pretty face," he joked, when he could speak again.

"So I see." She raised a dark brow before she slid into the passenger seat. Was she...flirting with him? *No, don't be ridiculous, you're seeing what you want to see.*

"So, how come you moved here? Where did you move from?"

"New Y-Orleans. I came from New Orleans," he said, trying to cover up the fact that he almost said where he was actually from. He was going to have to be careful with what he told her. He didn't want to lie to her, but he also didn't want her guessing who he was then being horrified that he had moved across the country in the hopes of starting life afresh, with her.

"Ooh, that sounds awesome. I would love to go to New Orleans. I'd love to explore the spiritual and voodoo culture, but don't tell my parents that. I mean, uh, never mind."

"You're worried about what your parents think of you?" he asked, knowing this was a subject that would get her talking.

"No, not at all. Just because I live with them, doesn't mean I care what they think," she sulked. There was that bravado again. Why did she keep pretending to be someone he knew she wasn't? Unless he didn't know her at all?

"Just here on the left, thanks," she said, and he pulled over in front of her parents' house. They got out in silence, him extricating her bike from his back seat with a finesse even he was proud of.

"Thanks for the ride, I'll see you tomorrow."

"You bet, already looking forward to it," he replied, his voice gruff as the breeze blew her scent towards him. She smelled like spiced apples, the scent sweet and sinful. She gave him a delicate wave and then headed inside the small farmhouse. He stared at the building wondering which room was hers. If he waited long enough, would he see the light go on? *Okay, time to go, creeper...*

He headed back to the little house he was renting. He had moved most of his stuff in but was yet to finish unpacking and the garment bag full of glamorous outfits continued to be ignored. He couldn't face looking at them just yet.

Love Me Good

His phone rang and he pulled it out of his jeans pocket, frowning as he saw it was *Tammy* calling. Tammy had been his long-time girlfriend, now his ex. He canceled the call and a moment later a message came through.

Tammy: I'm sorry.

He scoffed. She was only sorry she was no longer in the Morgan family's fold.

Ben was a romantic and had always wanted to find that one person he could bare his soul to. He thought Tammy could be it and had finally opened up to her, the first person since his grandma passed. He had shared his secret. Had shown her what he enjoyed doing in his spare time. Showed her the outfits, told her about the performances.

But Tammy had only been with him for the status his family name brought, using him to claw her way to the top of the social ladder. It turned out she didn't care which Morgan brother was warming her bed, because she'd also been sleeping with Matt behind Ben's back, and took the first opportunity to reveal what Ben secretly did in his spare time.

Matt had wasted no time in using the information to hurt him, announcing it in front of two hundred of their closest friends and family at the Morgans' annual cookout.

Needless to say, their father hadn't been thrilled at the idea that his youngest son spent his spare time performing as an Elvis Presley tribute act. A damn good one, if Ben did say so himself but his father didn't care about that. It wasn't medicine, it wasn't academic, it was just entertainment. Therefore it wasn't going to be tolerated. His grandma had been right, they would never understand it, never accept him. His father mocked him in front of everyone, humiliating him as Matt and Tammy joined in the ridiculing along with their *esteemed* guests.

Ben had left the party, his family, and hadn't looked back.

He would feel bad about leaving but there was nothing in New York for him. Since his grandma died, he'd felt so alone. She was the one who truly understood him, who shared his passion for music and introduced him to Elvis Presley. She was the one who encouraged him to perform and supported him. She even came to a few shows, had been right there in the front row, cheering him on. When she died suddenly, Ben was bereft, devastated that his partner in crime had left him all alone in a family that he was so disconnected from.

Since the party, Ben hadn't performed. He had canceled upcoming shows, packed away all his outfits, guitars and ignored his socials. Every time he even thought about getting back on stage, he pictured the faces of those closest to him, laughing at him, mocking him and humiliation clenched his stomach tight.

Ben blocked Tammy's number and put his phone away, then grabbed a beer, and chopped some vegetables for Geralt, hiding them all over Geralt's cage so the little chonk would have to work for his treats. Ben ruffled his fluffy mane and Geralt did a little playful leap in the air.

He went back to his computer and settled himself down, ready to speak to the one person above all others who mattered to him. Although he had spent time with her tonight, she had been guarded and aloof, she wasn't *his* Kayleigh and he needed his fix.

GoodGirlKay: What's a gamer's favorite type of fish?

Ben snorted to himself; he loved it when she sent him lame jokes.

GreenEyedKing96: Dare I ask…what?
GoodGirlKay: COD.

GreenEyedKing96: Groan...

GoodGirlKay: You love it really.

GreenEyedKing96: You got me there xx

GoodGirlKay: How's your new job going?

GreenEyedKing96: Really good so far, got to meet the woman I'll be working with.

GoodGirlKay: Is she nice? Do I need to send the realm's toughest assassin to have words with her?

GreenEyedKing96: She's very nice...

GoodGirlKay: Oh?? Like in the dating sense?

Ben paused before replying, mulling over his response.

GreenEyedKing96: She's definitely going to be a distraction that's for sure.

There was a long pause where he saw those three dots that signaled she was typing, then they disappeared. They appeared again and then disappeared. Then nothing for a good five minutes and he wondered what she was doing.

GoodGirlKay: I'm not sure how I feel about you getting a girlfriend, who will I talk to until the sun comes up?

GreenEyedKing96: I don't think you need to worry about that just yet. Anyway no one could replace you xx

GoodGirlKay: Aw, you type the sweetest things.

Ben snorted again and went into his kitchen to grab a bag of chips and another beer. When he came back she had messaged again.

GoodGirlKay: What does she look like?

GoodGirlKay: Anything like me?

GoodGirlKay: Sorry, that sounded weird...

GoodGirlKay: Dang it.

GoodGirlKay: How do you delete a message you've sent?

Ben's smile split his face.

GreenEyedKing96: You can't. Enough about my

new co-worker. How was your day?

GoodGirlKay: Good. I've been back to work; I took a week's break after the attack-slash-most-humiliating moment of my life.

GreenEyedKing96: I missed you while you were gone. How was it being back at work?

GoodGirlKay: Good, nice to be back, I do love that place. And got to meet the new guy.

Ben paused, he wanted to ask what she thought but also felt like he might not have made the best impression on her so far. It would hurt his feelings if she then complained about him to himself.

Then again, he was a sadist at heart.

GreenEyedKing96: What was he like?

GoodGirlKay: So far so good…

Ben would take that, all was not lost. Maybe he could make his online best friend his best friend in real life too.

*

Chapter 5

Kayleigh headed into the bar the next morning with a bounce in her step that had been missing for a long while. Her new clothes had turned up by the time she got home yesterday, and she was loving her trendier style. There wasn't exactly a lot you could do to be rebellious in a small town, Kayleigh would take what she could at this stage, and that meant a brand-new look.

She had a nice chat with her King last night and was excited for Taylor to see her outfit today. And she was excited to see Ben's reaction to her outfit too.

When she arrived, Taylor let out a loud wolf-whistle that had Kayleigh flushing to her toes. She had never been the recipient of a wolf-whistle before.

"Dang, I don't know what's gotten into you, but I like peach-haired, leather-wearing Kayleigh," Taylor whooped. Kayleigh laughed, smoothing a hand self-consciously over her white lace crop top and leather pants.

"Don't be shy. Own it, sweetheart, you've let your she-wolf out and there ain't nothing wrong with that." Taylor winked at her, her grief forgotten for a moment. Then Kayleigh saw her eyes dip, her shimmer fade away, and she squeezed Taylor's arm in support. Taylor offered her a small smile, patted Kayleigh's hand and then left to go into the office.

Kayleigh had the morning shift, and she knew that Ben would be in later to work the afternoon and evening so they would cross over for a couple of hours. She would be lying if she said she hadn't chosen her outfit with him in mind: she wanted to impress him.

He intrigued her, and she couldn't deny the little thrill she got over the idea of seeing him later. He seemed like everything she wasn't, from so confidently talking to someone he didn't know, working the bar like a pro despite it being the first time he'd ever worked in one, right down to the smooth way he removed her bulky bike from his car. If that had been her, there would have been a lot of awkward fumbling and apologizing.

Well, not anymore now that Kayleigh 2.0 had the wheel. She had been Googling fun things to do in the area and making a list of activities to check out and goals she wanted to achieve. Because nothing said cool and spontaneous like list-making. Towards the top of said list, right under *begin your writing career*, was the pole dancing class. It seemed like an easy one to tick off, except when she grabbed her phone and tapped in the number, she couldn't bring herself to actually press the green 'call' button.

She figured she needed baby steps first, that was all.

Love Me Good

She'd changed her look, gotten new clothes, and there was finally someone in town who was new. Who hadn't gone to school with her. Someone who didn't know everything about her, who didn't have preconceptions about her. She could start fresh with Ben and the thought excited her. Would he take her up on the offer to show him around town? She really hoped he would.

She bustled around the bar for a few hours, restocking liquor, checking on Taylor every now and then, as she sat seemingly just staring at the chair across her desk. It was a pretty slow morning, but it allowed Kayleigh to get some basic jobs crossed off. Then she heard the door to the bar open and flicked her eyes up to the mirrored wall that ran along the back of the bar and spotted Ben entering.

She fixed a sexy smirk on her face and turned to greet him.

*

"Kayleigh?" Ben choked out, hoping she didn't notice the strangled quality to his voice. He took in her white lacy top that didn't quite cover the red bra strap that peeked out. She turned around but not before he caught a glimpse of her perfectly sculpted ass in those tight leather pants, and his own pants had tightened in response.

She quirked her scarlet lips at him, all confidence so sexy that he half-expected her to stub out a cigarette and say, *"Tell me about it, stud."* Heat suddenly flared through him followed by an extreme sense of awareness.

She popped her hip to the side and placed her hand on it, her nails painted a deep red that matched her lips. "Yeah?"

He finally found his tongue. "Just didn't recognize you, that's all," he replied dumbly, heading over to stand next to her at the bar. He thought he saw something flash in her eyes, but she turned away.

"Well, now you know it's me."

"I sure do," he muttered.

Taylor came out from her office and greeted him. She raised her eyebrows at Ben and gestured towards Kayleigh. Ben looked at Kayleigh then back to Taylor, not understanding what Taylor was doing. Taylor rolled her eyes then mouthed something at him he couldn't make out, forming a heart shape with her fingers. "What?" he asked.

"Huh?" Kayleigh spun around.

"I, uh, decided now we have a little team, we should do team meetings. You two grab a booth and I'll get a notepad," Taylor said, glaring daggers at Ben who had no idea what just happened.

"Team meetings?" Kayleigh asked, but Taylor had already darted off.

"After you." Ben gestured to the booth and Kayleigh walked over and dropped down on one side. He figured it would be weird to sit next to her, so he slid across to the seat opposite. There was a moment of palpable tension as their eyes connected over the table, then Taylor joined them.

"Now, this is our first official team meeting, whoop!" Taylor smiled and Kayleigh giggled, her dimples deepening in her cheeks and Ben struggled to tear his eyes away. "I want to open up the floor to, firstly, welcome Ben to the team, hopefully all the drama hasn't scared you off?"

Ben shook his head.

"Good, it's not usually like that, I promise. Secondly, this is a place where we can talk about any ideas you have to drive customers into the bar. Anything you think this place is missing…Ooh, karaoke!" Taylor scribbled on her notepad.

Ben thought for a moment. "Do you do trivia nights here?"

Kayleigh shook her head.

"That feels like a good place to start. You could theme them, you know, movies, music, geography, that kind of thing. Also, it feels like a miss that there's no mechanical bull here."

"I like it, I like it. I wasn't expecting you to have ideas as you only started this week, but I'm impressed." Taylor continued scribbling furiously. At Taylor's praise Kayleigh frowned at him and he couldn't work out how he'd annoyed her.

"Also, along the line of the karaoke nights you could do themed ones like…Whitney Houston night, or Beyoncé night or," He cleared his throat which suddenly grew tight. "Elvis night?"

"I'm loving this, yes Ben!"

"I maybe have an idea," Kayleigh spoke hesitantly.

"Yeah?"

"We do Ladies' Nights but, um, they're for straight couples. We could maybe try, erm, doing like, an LGBTQIA series of them. There are other people looking for relationships and love, and this would make the bar stand out. It's a safe place for the community to come and not be judged and just be…accepted." Kayleigh wouldn't meet their eyes, just picked at the edge of the table that was lifting.

"That's a brilliant idea, Kayleigh," Ben replied.

"Yeah, I never knew you felt that way," Taylor said, staring at Kayleigh like she was suddenly seeing something she hadn't noticed before. "That is a fantastic idea, and we'll look to get those planned right away."

Kayleigh nodded, a small smile playing at her lips. When the meeting finished, Taylor went back into her office a little ball of excitement. Kayleigh escaped back to the bar to serve one of the locals and Ben followed her.

"That was a really good idea by the way. Well done for speaking up," he said.

She raised her dark eyebrows. "I'm sorry?"

His pulse pounded as her expression slipped into a cool mask. "Uh, well done for, ya know, demanding inclusivity? When someone stands up to demand inclusivity for others the world becomes a better place. But I can only imagine how nerve-racking it is to put yourself out there like that."

She took a step towards him. "And why would that be scary for me?"

Ben began sweating in places he didn't know he could sweat. "Because you're fighting for your community and in some small towns like this a lot of people wouldn't necessarily consider that a good thing."

"My community?"

"I thought…aren't you a lesbian?"

He panicked at her silence. "I…okay this isn't going how I planned. I just meant to say that I thought you had a great idea, and I think including all communities is extremely important so I'm dedicated to doing whatever we can all do together to make this happen."

She squinted at him but her shoulders dropped and she let out the air he didn't realize she had been holding.

"Are we cool?" he asked, scared of her answer.

"Sorry, you're right. Not everyone is accepting, and I wasn't sure which side of the fence you were going to fall on."

"The side of basic human decency? The bar is pretty low for that, huh?" he joked, nudging her shoulder until a small smile and those adorable dimples appeared.

"Wait, how did you know I like women?"

Shit, how did he explain that? Luckily, they were saved by Taylor coming back out to the bar and going over the dates of events with them that she had already planned. Once she left, they settled into a routine of Kayleigh showing him how to make some of the more advanced cocktails. Ben made her giggle by juggling some bottles and shocked himself by not dropping any. The afternoon picked up and they moved around each other in sync until the sun set and the moon rose high in the sky.

As the bar became more packed, the heat rose until Ben was stripping off his denim jacket and stuffing it up under the bar. He felt eyes on him, stroking over his back, but when he turned around, Kayleigh was busy serving more patrons. Taylor stepped in to help them out and it was pretty crammed behind the bar, so much so that Ben and Kayleigh kept brushing up against each other. He would stare down at her as she peeked up at him from under her lashes and his heart would do a little flip in his chest, until he reminded himself that it was *never gonna happen…*

As the evening wore on and the customers slowly left, something occurred to Ben.

"Didn't your shift finish like, three hours ago?" he asked, sidling up to Kayleigh.

She shrugged, wiping down the bar. "Figured you needed a hand since it was so busy."

"As nice as that is, you can go home. I'll be fine."

Her brows dipped in adorably. "Are you trying to get rid of me?"

"Never. I just figured you had something better to do than help me out."

"Never," she quipped, and he fought the smirk

working its way onto his face. "Besides there's a ton of cute guys here tonight and I'm feeling flirty."

He choked on the air leaving his lungs. "Isn't that a little mean? To tease them with something they can't have?"

One of her brows winged up in a manner that he found far too sexy. "Who says they can't have?"

"Because…you prefer women…right?"

"Not all the time. I'm bisexual, Ben." She smiled at him in that *aren't you silly* way.

A rushing sound filled Ben's ears, his heart pounding in his chest. Something unfurled in his chest. *Hope.*

"Oh, that's cool," was all he could say.

"But you're right, I should get going. See ya tomorrow," she said, giving him a pinkie wave and with a toss of her peachy hair she was gone.

Ben buzzed through the remainder of his shift, desperate for it to end so he could get home, log on to his computer and talk to her again. Because now, he had hope.

*

Chapter 6

GreenEyedKing96: I've missed you.
GoodGirlKay: It's only been 12 hours?!
GreenEyedKing96: Not the point. Tell me a joke?
GoodGirlKay: Sigh. What does a gamer use to make bread?
GreenEyedKing96: His console?
GoodGirlKay: If you're not going to take this seriously...
GreenEyedKing96: Ha, I'm sorry. I don't know, what does a gamer use to make his bread?
GoodGirlKay: Nope, you've ruined it #sadface
GreenEyedKing96: Noooo, please??
GreenEyedKing96: Come on, Kay pleeeeaaasssseeee?
GoodGirlKay: Fine.
GoodGirlKay: Ninten-dough
GreenEyedKing96: Baha, that was awful.

GreenEyedKing96: I loved it, thank you.

GoodGirlKay: How's the job going?

GreenEyedKing96: Good, I'm really enjoying it.

GoodGirlKay: I don't think you told me what it was you were doing?

GreenEyedKing96: It's just a bartending job.

GoodGirlKay: Oh wow, we're twinning? LOVE IT.

GreenEyedKing96: I figured you would.

GoodGirlKay: I bet you get a ton of tips, all the ladies all over you…

GreenEyedKing96: Snort, no. Besides, there's only one I want…

GoodGirlKay: Really?

GoodGirlKay: Who's the lucky girl?

GreenEyedKing96: Doesn't matter. How's your writing going?

GoodGirlKay: Psh, don't change the subject!

GreenEyedKing96: Now, who's changing the subject?

GoodGirlKay: Okay, you wanna play hardball – I see you Mr. King. Writing's meh…

GreenEyedKing96: Have you not been doing any?

GoodGirlKay: Nope.

GreenEyedKing96: How come?

GoodGirlKay is typing…

Pause.

GoodGirlKay is typing…

Pause.

GreenEyedKing96: Kay?

GoodGirlKay: Because what's the point? It doesn't go anywhere!

GreenEyedKing96: But you could make it go somewhere; your stories are amazing!

GoodGirlKay: You're my friend, you have to say that.

GreenEyedKing96: Actually being behind a keyboard means the anonymity would make it easier to lie to you but I'm telling you the truth. You aren't objective…

GoodGirlKay: But…

GreenEyedKing96: STILL TYPING HERE

GoodGirlKay: Sorry…

GreenEyedKing96: You aren't objective…you're too close to your work to be able to view it objectively, you're extra critical. As someone who has read your work, it's fantastic and it's a real shame it's not out there in the world.

GoodGirlKay: Dang, you're sweet.

GreenEyedKing96: I know.

GoodGirlKay: Okay fine, let's say I believe you. Let's say I AM actually good…how does someone like me go about putting this out there? It's so stupid, no one would take me seriously and I don't even have the guts to do it. I'm too scared.

GreenEyedKing96: So?

GoodGirlKay: So…?

GreenEyedKing96: Be scared…

GreenEyedKing96: …and do it anyway.

GoodGirlKay: That's easy for you to say…#sulks

GreenEyedKing96: Oh trust me, it really isn't.

GoodGirlKay: Anyway, so that's where I'm at.

GoodGirlKay: Now, I have reserved the right to change the subject.

GreenEyedKing96: No, no. We're not done with your thing!

GoodGirlKay: Well that's as much as we're going to discuss today.

GoodGirlKay: Who. Is. She.

GreenEyedKing96: #mansigh

GoodGirlKay: Aha! You're a man…

GreenEyedKing96: Yes I am. You knew that, right?
GoodGirlKay: *Sniffs* Maybe.
GreenEyedKing96: You so did.
GoodGirlKay: Yes, I did but I just wanted to highlight that's how little I know about you. I mean other than you just started a bartending job, your family sucks and we agree which Tarantino films are the best #deathproof4life and which were just meh.
GreenEyedKing96: #longlivePulpFiction…
GoodGirlKay: You know loads about me and I don't really know anything about you?
GreenEyedKing96 is typing…
GoodGirlKay: Should we do a video chat one day?
GoodGirlKay: I think we should do a video chat.
Pause.
GreenEyedKing96: Ah, sorry someone just turned up at my house. Talk later! Xx
GreenEyedKing96 has left the chat.
GoodGirlKay: …bye?
GoodGirlKay: Well, I guess now I know you live in a house…

*

Kayleigh pushed away from her computer feeling more confused than ever over her online friend. Every time she mentioned the possibility of them chatting over video or even a voice call, King got cagey and eventually logged off. What was his deal? She thought they were close enough, she thought they were friends and although they had met online, surely they had built a strong enough bond that the next logical step was meeting?

"So what gives, dammit!" she huffed and spun around in her chair. Her phone pinged and she looked across to her bed where she had flung the device when she came home. Her screen flashed and she hauled herself to her feet and picked up the phone. She tapped to open her new message:

Ben: I know you offered to show me around town but there's something that I wanna do tomorrow, if you're game?

Excitement bubbled in her veins. Her fingers flew over the screen as she typed her reply but paused before hitting send. Maybe she shouldn't appear too eager? She locked her screen. Maybe leaving him on read for a little while was better, like playing it cool? *Oh God, you're not a teenager so stop acting like one. Reply confidently!* Kayleigh 2.0 piped up. She unlocked her screen and sent her reply.

Kayleigh: Sounds good, where do you wanna meet and are you gonna tell me what it is?

His reply came back equally fast, and she couldn't stop her cheesy grin.

Ben: I think it'll work better as a surprise. I'll drop you a pin, I'm working the bar in the morning for a couple of hours so let's meet at 2 if that works for you? Wear something you don't mind getting wet…

She gasped softly when his message came through. *Something you don't mind getting wet…*there was no way he meant anything by it and yet her mind filled with all sorts of images. She tried to keep a lid on her excitement, not wanting to read too much into it but the butterflies in her stomach were flapping violently.

Lila Dawes

It's not a date, it's just an outing between co-workers, he didn't say date.
She didn't care.

*

Chapter 7

Ben paced back and forth at the edge of the road, nibbling his already nibbled thumbnail. He pulled the digit away from his mouth, shaking it as a spot of blood appeared.

"Now you over-nibbled..." he grumbled, before sticking his thumb back in his mouth and sucking away the red droplet. Was this the most nervous he had ever been in his life? Maybe. Including the time he sold out one of the theaters in New York with his tribute act, stepping out on stage to 500 adoring Elvis fans only to completely freeze up the second the music started. A cold sweat broke out over his neck at the memory. Okay maybe he was *nearly* as nervous as then. Not only was this a date with Kayleigh but it was a chance for him to overcome a fear too. He wanted to push her—and himself—out of their comfort zones, and he genuinely wasn't sure how she would react.

He forced out a breath and continued his pacing until he heard a sound. He looked up, and in the distance he could see her silhouette, cycling closer until the wide smile on her face came into focus. His own smile tugged at the corners of his mouth until they gave in and he let it out full force. She giggled as she came to a stop next to him, her peach hair aflame around her, her cheeks flushed from the exercise and her eyes shining bright. She was…he had no words. She wore a plain white T-shirt that vee'd in the middle, giving him a tiny, tantalizing glimpse of cleavage, and navy shorts, which showcased her bronzed legs.

"Hi," she said shyly.

"Hi," he replied, annoyed he couldn't come up with anything smoother than that. He emulated Elvis, for fuck's sake, would The King have really just said *Hi* like a lame teenager?

"Have you been waiting long?" she asked.

He shrugged. "Nah, not really." *Still not the best conversationalist today, are we?* He gritted his teeth. "Did it take you long?"

"A bit longer than anticipated but I enjoyed the ride," she replied, hopping off her bike and standing next to him. The sun bounced off her features, illuminating her skin and he found himself leaning towards her.

"Are you okay?" she asked, regarding him quizzically.

He snapped out of it. "Uh, yeah. Anyway, let's get a move on while the sun is still high, it's this way." He gestured into the woods, and she looked behind him before sliding her eyes to his, nibbling her lip.

"The woods?"

"Yeah. Is that okay?"

"Sure…" she said, and he watched her bravado slide into place.

"I won't let anything happen to you." He was trying to hold back the extreme fierceness that tried to slip out.

She smiled at him and then turned her bike, pushing it into the woods and walking along next to it. They began their walk in silence, Ben racking his brain for something to say, the organ always seemed to go quiet around Kayleigh, like she stunned it into silence. He needed to think of something to say so that she didn't think he was luring her here with nefarious intentions. *Who even says nefarious anymore?*

"So, how long have you worked at The Bucket?" Ben asked.

"About eighteen months now."

"You planning on staying there?"

She shrugged. "There aren't many career opportunities in a small town, even if I traveled to the next town over. I'm just grateful my parents are letting me live at home still until I can figure something out."

"You like living with them?"

"Yeah," she shrugged. "We have a great relationship, and it beats being lonely. It's nice having someone to come home to and talk about your day with, you know? Do you get on with your family?"

"Uh, no," he replied. She glanced at him when he didn't elaborate but he didn't really want to go into that trauma right now. Besides he was focused on her today.

"What about hobbies then, what do you like?" he asked.

"Um, I like music."

"What kind?"

"I'm a bit of a pop princess I guess, but I do like some alternative stuff too."

"What else? What other hobbies?" He wanted to get her talking about her writing, and see if she opened up any more about that. After their chat online last night he was determined to encourage her to put her stories out there in the world, the gaming community deserved her interwoven plots with twists and turns at every corner. It was a crime that these games didn't exist but more than that, it made him sad that she lacked the courage to try.

"Exercising, does that count?"

He laughed. "Yes, that counts but what else?"

She shrugged one shoulder and picked at some lint on her T-shirt. "I do a bit of writing."

Jackpot! "Oh yeah?" He tried to act calmly but inside he was squealing like a kid that she had opened up to him. "Anything in particular?"

"Just journaling."

Hmm. "Would you ever publish anything?"

Kayleigh snorted. "This town already has one published author, Christy Lee."

"Is there a rule against having more than one?"

"I guess not, I just feel like the chances would be pretty slim."

He could sense her clamming up, she avoided his stare, shifting uncomfortably. It was enough though, she had shared something, and he wouldn't push her for more at this stage. It would come with time, he was just impatient.

"What about you?" she asked, pinning him with her soft blue eyes.

"I also like music but I like older stuff, more blues and Motown," he said.

"Ooh, an old soul, huh?"

"I guess so." Now it was Ben's turn to feel uncomfortable. He always feared people's reactions to his

Love Me Good

music taste. It wasn't that he was embarrassed exactly, it was just that you didn't find many people his age that listened to music from sixty years ago. It was all techno and rap and hip hop. God, how old did he sound?

She peeked up at him from under her fluttering bangs. "Who's your favorite artist?"

No way could he say his true answer, so he came up with the next one in his mind. "Nina Simone."

"Never heard of her."

He turned to her, horrified and she giggled. "But I do like some Motown stuff, like Etta James and Aretha Franklin," she added.

He smiled. "Oh yeah?"

Kayleigh nodded, a sweet smile fighting its way across her lips. "Guess we have something in common then."

"We sure do." Ben couldn't tear his eyes away from her. That is, until he spotted the clearing up ahead in the trees. "We're here," he said, pointing towards the clearing. When they walked through the parted trees, Kayleigh looked around and gasped.

"Oh my God! How have I lived here my whole life and didn't know this existed?" Her eyes darted around, taking in the bright green of the trees that refused to succumb to early fall's embrace. The waterfall from the tops of the rocks that plummeted into the pond below. Bushes and flowers surrounded the pond, and birds tweeted nonstop. It was like a miniature tropical paradise. Ben had accidentally found it a few days ago while out exploring his new hometown.

"You really didn't know this was here?"

"Are you kidding? I would be here all the time if I did!" Kayleigh squealed and her joy had him chuckling. She let her bike drop into the grass and hurried over to the rocks, clambering over them to get better access to the water. The waterfall pounded into the mini lake but there was a decent space for swimming and Ben immediately began removing his socks and shoes.

"Shall we dive in?"

Kayleigh turned to him, her eyes on his feet before they slid up to his crotch where he began unbuttoning his khaki shorts. She swallowed and nodded before meeting his stare. He pulled his shorts down and stepped out of them, folding them up, not wanting to crease the material. She cleared her throat and turned away as he pulled his shirt over his head, folding that up too and placing it with his shorts.

He suddenly felt self-conscious. He wasn't buff and muscled like some of the guys he'd seen in town. Would she like his lean body? Did she like a beefier look on a man? His thoughts derailed when she pulled her T-shirt over her head and peered at him over her shoulder. The air left his lungs in a huff and his throat tightened, breathing impossible as she bent over and pulled her shorts down her legs, stepping out of them daintily.

She faced him in her two-piece white swimsuit decorated with little cherries that would be forever imprinted on his brain. She was too adorable and too sexy, the two aspects of her startling him as he realized she was the first woman who he just wanted to pull into a hug and then bend over the nearest thing he fucking could.

"Race you!" she shouted then cannonballed into the lake, astonishing him.

He laughed and ran over to the edge just in time to see her break the surface, water trickling down her fair skin. His gaze traced each drop as it disappeared back into the water about her shoulders.

Her arm hit the water, sending a wave towards him.

Love Me Good

"Come on!"

He laughed again at her glee before he dived in and came up next to her, splashing her. They played together, teasing each other. They grew competitive: who could hold their breath the longest? Who could swim the width the quickest? Who could perform the most dramatic dive? He disappeared under the water and tickled her legs and darted out of the way before she could kick at him. When he resurfaced, she pushed him back under, then he wrapped his arms around her waist and lifted her up, throwing her into the deeper end. Her peals of laughter only spurred him on until they were finally floating side by side, exhausted. The rush of water, the bird song and just being with her created the perfect moment.

"Thank you," she murmured.

He turned his head slightly to look at her. "For what?"

"For today, for not treating me like everyone else in this town, like I need to do you a favor. I've been struggling recently with life stuff and it's been nice forgetting who I used to be."

The thought of her struggling while he had no idea didn't sit well. "Used to be?" he asked, feeling his brow furrow at her words.

"I wasn't happy with who I was and I'm trying to be a new version of myself, a 'Kayleigh 2.0' if you will."

"Kayleigh 2.0, huh? What's different about her?"

Kayleigh considered that for a moment. "She's more confident, she won't be pushed around, and she takes control of what she wants."

"She sounds great, I can see why she exists. But how come those aren't previous Kayleigh traits?"

She swam upright and played with the water before shrugging.

He didn't want to push her, he just wanted to

understand more about her change. "OG Kayleigh was pretty cool too, ya know."

Her cute nose wrinkled. "You never properly met her."

His pulse pounded in his ears at his little slip up. "Uh…I've seen glimpses of her, and I liked what I saw. But so far, I'm just a fan of Kayleigh all round."

"All Kayleighs are fans of you too." She smiled shyly again. He loved that little peekaboo smile, especially as he watched a water droplet trickle down her face and land in the crease of her lip. He was suddenly desperate to pull her into his arms. He began to move towards her.

"Kayleigh 2.0 found something else she likes." She interrupted his maneuver, her head tilted back. He followed her stare and his stomach plummeted. There were two platforms overlooking the waterfall, one halfway up and one at the top. Both looked perfect for diving from, and that was exactly what he knew Kayleigh wanted to do but fear trapped him in place.

He shook his head. "No."

"Yes!" she cried and grabbed his arm, dragging him toward the edge of the lake. He was momentarily distracted when she vaulted out of the water and all her glorious skin was on spectacular display, wet and glistening.

"Come on, Ben!"

"Hang on a minute," he protested, desperately willing his erection away, especially in his swim shorts that would cling to his body the second he got out of the water. He turned away from her and pulled himself out of the lake, using the delay to rearrange his goods before turning back around. Steely resolve settled over her expression before she dragged him over to the waterfall and his heart practically leapt out of his chest.

He had never been afraid of falling before, not until two years ago when he fell off the front of the stage in a concert venue he'd played. He had raised his leg to place it on an amp he thought was at the edge of the stage but there was nothing there. The smoke machines and flashing lights made it impossible to see the edge and he tumbled straight off, breaking his ankle and two ribs. His stomach still turned every time he remembered the moment he realized he was falling and the helpless feeling that went with it.

After that he stuck to smaller venues, too terrified of the same thing happening. While a smaller crowd was intimate, he missed the buzz from hundreds of fans screaming for him, the energy the crowd gave him back was like a shot of heroin to the veins. He missed performing. A lot.

"Together?" Kayleigh asked, peering up at the highest platform.

"No way," Ben shook his head. He wasn't even going to try and style out his fear. No way could he get up that high. She was lucky he had gotten as far up these rocks as he had, and that was only because he had let her drag him there.

Kayleigh frowned at him. "You don't like heights?"

"It's not the fear of heights, it's the fear of falling. The weightless, flailing plummet that can only end in pain," he rasped. Was the air thinner up here? He was struggling to catch a breath all of a sudden.

"Okay, so not the top platform, but what about this one? It's only gonna be about fifteen feet? That's not too bad, think about all that cool water ready to catch you," she soothed, stroking her hand down his arm. She led him towards the edge and he let her, amazed he had even gotten as close as this. It was only because of her. He peeked over and shook his head, dropping her hand and retreating.

"Immediately no."

He hadn't meant to be funny but she laughed, the sound bubbling from her and he decided he needed to hear it all the time.

"Just hear me out," she said, catching his hand once again. "It's the falling you don't like but this is falling with *purpose*. That's different, right? This is deciding to fall for the sheer fun of falling. The thrill. The adrenaline rush that comes with being reckless, being a *rebel*. Don't you crave that? Can't you hear it calling out to you, begging you?" Her passion emanated from her and at that moment he could swear he did feel it calling to him, that adrenaline rush he was missing by not performing anymore was singing in his blood. Or was it her? Had she snuck her way inside, coursing through him? Her eyes bewitched him, her skin covered in delicious goosebumps he just wanted to lick away. His eyes dropped to her breasts, her nipples hard behind the cherry covered fabric and he forced himself to look away.

"Do you trust me?" she asked, holding out her hand.

He snorted. "Okay, *Aladdin*."

She giggled. "I'm being serious! Do you?"

He looked between her outstretched hand and the edge. Really it wasn't that far at all, he was being ridiculous. But he also wanted that feeling she mentioned, that was the feeling he got when he was on stage, and it had been so long that he craved it, like a part of his soul was missing. He also wanted to please her. He had always been a little bit of a people pleaser but to see that smile on her face and know he put it there? Hell yes.

"I won't let anything bad happen to you," she said, echoing his words from earlier.

Love Me Good

He stepped towards the edge, took her hand and together, they leapt.

He screamed all the way down.

The rush filled his brain, sent him high and when he resurfaced to find her giggling beside him, he whooped.

"Again!"

*

Chapter 8

"Hang out with me?"

Kayleigh looked up from the dishwasher to find Ben leaning over the bar, smiling at her. That smile she couldn't stop staring at during their non-date date where he hadn't kissed her despite all her signals. She could have been wearing a neon sign on her forehead that said *kiss me please, Ben!* and he wouldn't have noticed it.

She knew she should have made the first move, but she didn't have the guts to go for it. She nearly unleashed Kayleigh 2.0 but then thought that maybe he hadn't made a move because they worked together and he didn't want to make things awkward. Either way, she'd had more fun with him than she'd had in what felt like forever.

"Kayleigh?" He interrupted her thoughts.

She nodded to the dishwasher she was nearly finished

stacking. "I need to finish this."

"Okay, after then? It'll take like two seconds, and I've cleaned up everywhere else so we're done for the night," he said. Kayleigh glanced around seeing that he was in fact correct: everything was done. Taylor had left earlier. She was doing that more now, taking time back for herself. Kayleigh was really proud of her for that, even if it meant they spent less time together. Although maybe the time apart was helping, Kayleigh noticed she wasn't pining for the sassy redhead as bad as usual.

"Taylor said we could hang out here tonight," Ben sing-songed, arching a fuzzy brow and gesturing to the pool table.

"Fine," she conceded and nodded at the pool table. "Rack 'em."

She finished stacking the dishwasher in record time and came out from behind the bar carrying two bottles of beer to find Ben waiting for her, cue in hand.

"I figured you'd want the smaller one, because, ya know, you're teeny," he teased.

"I'm not teeny," she grumbled. That didn't sound like a compliment and goddamn him she wanted his compliments.

"Ladies first."

"But men just before," Kayleigh quipped.

Ben smirked then bent forward over the table, lining up his shot. He swung his arm back and an almighty *thwack* ricocheted around the room. The balls split off, rolling over the green felt and rebounding off the sides of the table. However none dropped into the pockets. With a smug grin Kayleigh strolled around to his side and hip-checked him out of the way before leaning over and sizing up her shot.

Being that she was so teeny she had to lean as far

forward as possible and there was a lot of shuffling and throat clearing behind her. She tapped the ball with the cue and it slid into the pocket with a gentle *swish*. She turned to find Ben watching her, his bright eyes glittering.

"What?"

More throat clearing. "Nothing, you just look *great* when you take a shot." He shot her a devilish smile. *Is he flirting?* She hated that she couldn't tell. Why was he so hard to read? The only way to find out is to respond and see what he did. When he lined up his next shot, her eyes were fixed to his crotch.

"Something caught your eye?" Those mint velvet eyes glittered again, this time with a quirked brow that was all kinds of sexy. Her brain short-circuited and she relied on a flirty pun to get her through. "I was just admiring your balls."

A poor excuse for a flirty pool pun, however Ben surprised her by barking out a laugh, a deep throaty rumble that culminated in a wicked smile, totally out of character for him and her knees knocked together. She discreetly grabbed the edge of the table for support. She liked flirting with this guy, it gave her the same feeling as GreenEyedKing96. Ben felt safe and although she hadn't known him long, he felt like an old friend.

"Touché." He dipped his pool cue at her in salute. She couldn't think of anything else to say so just took her turn. "Tell me something Kayleigh, do you like gaming?"

She fumbled her shot. "No, why?" she answered a little too quickly. Was it getting hot in here or was it just her and her lies? Why was she so afraid to admit she liked gaming? She had told him about her writing but didn't want to admit it was mostly gamer fanfiction. It was ridiculous but she just wanted him to think she was cool, and fanfiction was definitely not cool.

Love Me Good

"No? Hmm." His eyes swung to her, squinting like he didn't believe her one bit. He leaned his cue against the table and pulled his sweater over his head, the T-shirt underneath getting caught and riding up with it, exposing salacious inches of taut skin and a hint of happy trail that had the grip on her cue tightening. He tossed his sweater onto the nearest table to straighten his T-shirt and it was then that she saw the *Byte Me* on it and she honestly thought she died and went to heaven. *He's a gamer too?*

"Are you sure about that?" he asked. She didn't reply and he took her silence as affirmative. "That's a shame. I love gaming and thought I sensed a vibe." He lifted a shoulder, all *eh, what you gonna do?* And she suddenly wanted to reveal how much they had in common.

"I love gaming," she blurted out. "My favorite is Queen's Ransom, the quest game."

Ben's lip quirked up in a smile. "There we go. That wasn't so hard, was it?" He lifted his cue and took another shot, the muscles in his forearm popping as he forced the cue between his fingers.

Lord, have mercy.

He looked at her and nibbled his lip. "Why did you say you didn't like gaming?"

She swallowed thickly. "Because I wanted you to think I'm cool." Dang it, between them beer and Ben had loosened her tongue.

"Even though we've hung out a couple times now and if I didn't like you, I wouldn't?"

She nodded.

"Even though I said I liked gaming too?"

She shrugged, feeling a little helpless at his probing. She was so used to forcing herself not to talk about her hobbies that it was second nature to deny them.

"Maybe I should just be myself instead of pretending

to be someone else," she whispered. When the silence stretched on, she lifted her eyes and met his stare. Connection sizzled between them, and she fought the shiver that tried to slowly trek its way down her spine.

"That sounds good to me," he husked.

Her vulnerability crawled through her skin to an unbearable degree. "Tell me a secret, something no one else knows?" she begged, needing him to be vulnerable too and even the power balance.

She thought he would deny her. Why would anyone give up a secret to a new friend? Then his mouth tipped to the side in contemplation before he offered her a genial smile, the corners of his stunning green eyes crinkling.

"I guess fair's fair. I've only ever slept with one woman," he said. She nearly spat her drink out. *I mean…same*, she thought to herself.

"Thoughts?" he asked when she realized she'd been quiet. She mulled his words over, wondering at the fuzzy feeling deep in her belly and the tingles branching out from her chest at the thought of him only being with one woman.

"Admirable."

He laughed. She loved the way his deep rippling baritone echoed around the empty bar and she decided it was her favorite sound. He dipped his head and then looked up at her, a mischievous gleam in his eyes that was ever so charming. *How had he only had one woman? They must be throwing themselves at him.*

"Now you," he said.

She spluttered. "I already went!"

"You admitted you liked gaming, so did I. Then you asked for a secret and I gave you one, so the way I see it, we're two for one on this vulnerable confessions thing."

He sidled over to her and perched against the table, putting them at roughly the same height. "Care to even the score?" His scent and heat invaded her space, driving her senses wild.

"I signed up for pole dancing but I'm too scared to go," she blurted out.

He arched a brow and shifted slightly. "Why?"

"What do you mean, why? Look at me," she gestured to herself. His eyes ran a lazy trail from head to foot, lingering over her hips and she took another pull from her beer to refresh her suddenly parched mouth.

"I try not to, but I can't seem to help myself," he sighed.

"I'm not sexy and I couldn't be if I tried," she snorted.

He choked on his beer before eyeing her again. "Dance for me."

Her pulse pounded in her ears at his words. "What?"

"Right now."

She scoffed. "Hell no, besides there's no pole!"

"You don't need the pole. Come on, what's the worst that could happen? You'll feel embarrassed or it could get awkward? We'll both get over it. No one will die."

No one will die, her brain repeated.

This was very true. How was she actually considering this? What was it about him that had her throwing caution into the wind every time he asked her to?

"Just dance like the bad girl you are."

The way he said *bad girl* had her blood heating, nerves and impulses zapping through her. Was she really going to do this? This would be the craziest thing she'd ever done. But if she couldn't dance for him alone then how could she do it in a room full of other people? She took a large swig of her beer and then tentatively set it on the edge of the pool table. She took his cue from him, their eyes locked together as she tossed it onto the table. Was she crazy or did she see something dangerous in those jade depths?

He widened his legs, giving her access to get closer. An invitation and she accepted, gratefully. She stepped between his legs, putting them face to face. Nose to nose. Mouth to mouth. Barely a whisper apart.

"Just imagine some sensual music," he whispered, his eyes on her lips and she felt his breath like a caress over her skin, her eyes nearly rolling back in her head.

"Like what?"

"It's your dance, bad girl. It can be whatever you want it to be. What song is playing for you right now?"

She thought about it then; *"Down In Mexico*, The Coasters."

"*Deathproof*," he breathed.

Her eyes snapped to his. He knew that? "Butterfly. She's so sensual, there's this scene..." Her words stuttered from her, not making sense but her brain was powering down, her body gearing up to take over. Her fight or flight instinct was kicking in.

He shook his head, chuckling, the sound dark and promising. "Goddamn I'm so happy I'm a Tarantino fan."

"You are?"

He nodded, then pressed his finger to her lip, ending her stalling.

Silence.

Then the song began in her head and her hips took over. She rolled, she writhed and inched herself closer and closer until she rubbed against him. She heard him swallow, felt him tense as she moved over him. Then she felt him harden.

The power shot through her veins and her inhibitions

disappeared along with Kayleigh 2.0 until she was just *Kayleigh*. She grabbed his hands and ran them over her body, around her hips, under the material of her shirt and across her stomach. His hard calloused hands gliding across her soft skin had her biting her lip. She removed his hands from under her shirt and trailed them up to graze the sides of her breasts. His breathing grew labored in her ear and he brought one hand up to clasp her throat as his lips brushed her ear, his hot breath teasing the shell before his tongue slid along the sensitive skin and she quivered in pleasure. She bent at the waist and rocked her hips before she stood up, flipping her hair back and eyeing him over her shoulder.

Ben spun her around and covered her mouth with his, slanting his soft lips over hers, plumping her, tasting her. His tongue slid into her mouth, and she opened eagerly to let him in. When he stroked deftly against her, she tunneled her hand into his thick hair and gripped tightly. He huffed against her lips and she swallowed his moan as she sucked his tongue, hard.

Kayleigh pressed herself against him, desperate to feel him everywhere. He licked into her mouth again and again, teasing her and retreating, forcing her to chase him, making her come to him and take what she wanted. He was an expert kisser, hot, gentle but demanding and she collapsed against him, unable to hold herself up on her wobbling legs anymore.

Her core pulsed insistently, begging for attention and she shifted her hips against him, desperate to grind against his hardness while he worked her mouth so perfectly. Then he pulled away and the lights of the bar, the pool table, came back into focus but her world was blurry, shaken to its core by his kiss. She stared up at him dumbly, his mouth was puffy and swollen, and she was eager for another taste. His eyes glazed over, and his slicked back hair now stuck out at odd angles. Had she done that?

He tucked her hair behind her ear and framed her face with his hands and when he finally spoke, his tone was all gravel. "I think that answers your question on being sexy." He ran his thumb over her bottom lip then turned away, picking up his cue and potting the last two balls before she could even blink.

"Come on, let's get you home," he said, not meeting her eyes before he took their beer bottles and tossed them. Then he was leading her outside, locking up the bar and shoving her bike into the trunk of his car. And she was sitting inside wondering what the hell had happened in the last two minutes?

He didn't say anything the entire drive to hers and she didn't know whether it was a good thing or not. She had been vulnerable and opened up to him, and he had kissed her.

He kissed *her*.

When he pulled up outside her house, he once again removed her bike from his car in one smooth motion and then dipped his head, pressing his lips to her cheek. His stubble teased her and she realized her cheeks were stinging slightly from where it had rubbed against her in their make out session.

"Goodnight, bad girl," he murmured.

*

Chapter 9

Working alongside Ben was getting harder by the day. Seeing those green eyes watching her so intently and the way his lush mouth kicked up on one side in a sinful lip curl had hunger crawling through her. She had tasted that mouth; she knew exactly what delights it could deliver. She was eager for more but he hadn't made any moves.

Sometimes she thought he was flirting, like when he would move behind her in the cramped bar, his hands on her hips, shifting her to the side, his lips by her ear making goosebumps burst to life across her skin. Time slowed as she looked at him over her shoulder, their eyes connecting, heat sizzling between them. During those moments, the sounds of the bar vanished and all that could be heard was the heavy panting of their breaths. Then he would remove his hands and the world came back into focus with a harsh jolt.

Kayleigh decided that he was too sexy for a bartender. The way he laughed with patrons, the strength he exhibited when changing a keg over, right down to the flick of his wrist when he took the top off a bottle of beer, making every flex of his forearms downright obscene.

He had an energy, the elusive X factor that you couldn't name, that made people gravitate towards him. Kayleigh watched it happen every shift and each time tried to tamp down the jealousy she felt clawing at her insides. She watched him flirt harmlessly and charm both men and women alike, just like he did with her. Which is what made her decide that, despite their kiss, she was firmly entrenched in the friend zone and that felt like a bigger blow than realizing she and Taylor would never happen.

As though her thoughts summoned her, Taylor appeared next to her, her emerald eyes sparkling in the light. It had been four weeks since her nasty ex had died, and Kayleigh was pleased to see Taylor was doing better each day.

"Everything cool?" Kayleigh asked, cataloguing Taylor's features and waiting for the pang of longing that usually knocked her off her feet every time she saw the woman, but this time it never came.

"I decided to bring the bar into the twenty-first century and set up an Instagram account. I posted about the LGBTQIA nights coming up and it's had a ton of engagement and shares and people messaging asking for more dates!" Taylor bounced up and down and did a little wiggle before pulling Kayleigh into a hug and spinning her around. When they turned, Kayleigh noticed Ben was staring at them, his hands on his hips, a frown puckering his forehead that didn't leave until she had extricated herself from Taylor's gangly limbs.

"That's amazing!" Kayleigh squealed. Ben came over to join them and Taylor reiterated the news before turning back to Kayleigh.

"Thank you so much for the suggestion, I can't believe it had never occurred to me to do this before so thank you for bringing it to my attention," Taylor said, tucking a strand of hair behind Kayleigh's ear. The motion was something that, a few months ago, would have rendered Kayleigh speechless, but now it smacked of sisterly affection and Kayleigh…wasn't mad about it. Was she finally getting over Taylor?

A low growl distracted Kayleigh from her analysis and she flicked her eyes to Ben who had a slightly feral look in his eyes that Kayleigh also decided she wasn't mad about.

"Excuse me," he grunted before heading down the corridor to the kitchen.

"I'm so proud of you, sweetheart. Watching you over the last eighteen months and seeing the woman you're becoming makes me so happy," Taylor said, distracting her.

"Oh my God, why are you doing this to me?" Kayleigh asked, emotion clogging her throat as the words sank in.

Taylor laughed. "Because everyone deserves to know how amazing they are. I want nothing but happiness for you. You're like my little sister, you know?"

Kayleigh hugged her again, words failing her at Taylor's sweetness, and again, it didn't hurt that Taylor confirmed exactly the type of relationship she felt they had. If anything, Kayleigh thought she was right. She had always found Taylor gorgeous and admired what a strong woman Taylor was but is that all her feelings were? Pure admiration and idolization? The more she examined them the more Kayleigh acknowledged that Taylor *did* feel like her big sister, she certainly looked up to her in that way and their relationship was something that she would forever cherish.

When they broke away Ben returned, looking a little grouchy and definitely stomping his feet. Taylor hurried back into her office but returned before Kayleigh could question Ben on his sudden mood change.

"So, tomorrow is Christy and Dean's wedding reception, don't forget I need you both here a little earlier to start setting up," she said, flicking through the planner she held. Dean was Taylor's stepbrother and he was marrying Taylor's best friend, Christy who had come back to town a couple of years ago.

Kayleigh whistled low. "Wow, that's come around quick."

Ben turned away to grab a beer for Porter, one of the regulars.

"Doesn't feel like it," Taylor muttered.

A pang hit Kayleigh as she realized that Beau would be at the wedding as he was Dean's best man, and it would be the first time Taylor saw him since he left after the attack. Although Taylor tried to hide her feelings, she shone a little less brightly than usual in the recent weeks and it had been painful to see.

"Is Beau definitely coming back for it?" she asked hesitantly. Although Taylor just declared them sisters, they never really talked about anything personal, and Kayleigh didn't know if she was overstepping any boundaries.

"As far as I know. I bet he'll look good in his tux, the sexy prick," Taylor grumbled.

"I'm sure you'll look just as stunning in your dress, and

you'll make him wish he'd never left," Kayleigh replied.

"Thanks, girl," Taylor said. When Ben rejoined them, she added, "Because you're both working earlier tomorrow I want you to take the following evening off, that's non-negotiable."

Ben smiled and mock-saluted. "Yes, ma'am."

Kayleigh managed to tear her eyes from his wicked smile long enough to nod her head in agreement. The rest of their shift passed by uneventfully and Kayleigh was a little surprised when Ben dropped her off at home and just said goodbye. He didn't talk about anything other than general bar chitchat, there were no deep and meaningful conversations, no sharing of vulnerable secrets, no references to their previous day date or even their kiss. She was definitely in the friend zone. That bothered her so much more than she had thought it would. *What gives?*

After chatting with her parents briefly, Kayleigh went to her room and switched on her computer, the device whirring away comfortingly as she waited for her King to come online so she could ask him the question she'd been psyching herself up to ask.

GoodGirlKay: Would you maybe read my newest story? It feels like something is missing but I don't know what?

GreenEyedKing96: Absolutely, can't wait! What's this one about?

GoodGirlKay: It's a Romeo & Juliet retelling, but in gamer form with quests obviously.

GreenEyedKing96: You had me at Romeo…

GoodGirlKay: Haha, I hope it translates well, some people might think it's weird?

GreenEyedKing96: Then those people are stupid.

Question, do they end up together?

GoodGirlKay: I'm not sure yet, that's the bit that's missing.

GreenEyedKing96: So, no ending? What's going to happen to my sense of closure?

GoodGirlKay: We'll discuss it together and decide what the best ending is.

GreenEyedKing96: Surely you can't kill them? How is that a happy ending? It's not romantic at all and you know people love a romance!

GoodGirlKay: But if they stay alive there's no sacrifice. And isn't it romantic that they'll be together in death?

GreenEyedKing96: Absolutely not.

GoodGirlKay: Okay, well this is why I have you, to help me with these problems.

GreenEyedKing96: That's all I'm good for?

GoodGirlKay: There's other things…

GreenEyedKing96: Such as?

GoodGirlKay: It's a great boost when you laugh at my lame jokes…

GreenEyedKing96: They're not lame, they're my favorite part of the day. What else?

GoodGirlKay: Ummmm, you pump me up and make me feel happy.

Pause.

GreenEyedKing96: Do I make you feel anything else?

Kayleigh's heart thudded in her chest and her cheeks grew hot. Of course, he made her feel other things, but is that what he was getting at? Was he finally taking this somewhere *deeper*? Why did Ben suddenly pop into her head?

"Okay, okay, relax. Think of what to reply…" She cracked her knuckles and her fingers hovered over the keyboard.

GoodGirlKay: Yes.

His reply was instantaneous, the quickest he had *ever* replied.

GreenEyedKing96: What do I make you feel?

Kayleigh sucked in a breath, her stomach fluttering and her core heating up. Were they actually about to do this?

GoodGirlKay: Needy.
GreenEyedKing96: Fuck Kay.

Kayleigh started panicking, thinking she had taken this in the completely wrong direction versus what he said. She began typing her apology but his next message had her fingers stilling and a squeak slipped from her.

GreenEyedKing96: I'm so hard.

No. Way.

Okay, this was happening, all systems go. She began typing but stopped, began again and stopped again. She didn't know what to say.

GreenEyedKing96: Don't leave me hanging…

She needed to engage Kayleigh 2.0. She would have the confidence to continue what Actual Kayleigh really wanted. She took a deep breath, her eyes fluttering closed, channeling Kayleigh 2.0's confidence and when she opened them, she knew exactly what to do.

GoodGirlKay: Are you touching yourself?

GreenEyedKing96: Yes.
GoodGirlKay: How does it feel?
GreenEyedKing96: So good, though not nearly as good as if you were here…
GoodGirlKay: What are you thinking about?
GreenEyedKing96: You.
GoodGirlKay: What am I doing in these thoughts?
GreenEyedKing96: On your knees, sucking me, begging me.
GoodGirlKay: Begging you to what?
GreenEyedKing96: Fuck you.
GreenEyedKing96: Hard.
GreenEyedKing96: I want to feel how wet you are for me.
GreenEyedKing96: I want to make you scream.
GreenEyedKing96: I want you to come so hard I feel every flutter around my dick, gripping me tight and then you take everything I have to give.

His messages came fast, each one driving her need higher and higher, and she didn't get a chance to reply, just let him keep going, getting out everything he wanted to say. There was a pause where he probably waited for her response, but she didn't know what to say.

She didn't need words, she needed actions. Emboldened by his words she typed out her reply.

GoodGirlKay: Video chat?

"Kayleigh!" her father shouted up the stairs and Kayleigh yelped, leaping back from her computer like she'd been caught doing exactly what she was doing.

"Yeah?" she shouted back, her voice strained.

"Your Gammy is on the phone, she wants to talk to

you!"

Kayleigh sighed, then pushed away from her computer and went downstairs, hoping her cheeks weren't as red as they felt. She chatted to Gammy briefly, promising to come over and see her soon. When they hung up, she went back upstairs to her computer, eager to pick up where she and King left off and see what his reply was.

An ache pierced her chest when she looked at the screen and saw one new message.

GreenEyedKing96 has left the chat.

*

Chapter 10

The following day when Kayleigh arrived at the bar to prep for the wedding reception, Ben was already there and looking fine as all hell in his black pants and black button down, his blond hair slicked back, and a slight scruff on his jaw where he hadn't shaved.

"Hey you," she said, trying to walk towards him on jelly legs, ready for his smile to send her into a melty puddle of need.

"Hey," he replied, glancing briefly over his shoulder but not meeting her eyes.

"Everything okay?" she asked, her brows pulling together in concern. His back was tense, the muscles rigid beneath his shirt and when his eyes swiveled to her again she thought she saw guilt shining back at her but she must be imagining it. Either way, he definitely seemed off.

"Yep, you?"

She nodded and he turned away. She frowned at his back before retreating to Taylor's office to store her bike helmet as usual.

"Did you open up this morning?" she asked when she re-entered the main bar.

"Yeah, had to let the caterers in early and start setting up."

"Guess Taylor really trusts you to give you a key now, congrats. It's hard to earn her trust, she must see something special in you."

Ben turned to face her, his expression unreadable. He opened his mouth, but no words came out and then he just lifted one shoulder in that casual shrug he was so fond of doing.

"I see something special too." She couldn't stop the words from tumbling out. Kayleigh 2.0 was clearly in charge without her permission. What was she even saying? They barely knew each other but she couldn't help feeling a deeper connection, like she'd known him so much longer.

He rubbed the back of his neck, his eyes avoiding hers. "Uh, thanks."

She spun away, embarrassment flaming her cheeks as she digested what she'd just said to him.

"Right then, I'll put these up." She grabbed a floral garland and headed towards the small stage in the corner. They moved around each other in sync, him tackling all the decorations that required being hung up high, clambering up the ladder with ease, his fear of falling not stopping him, and her sticking to all those that were displayed lower down.

When Taylor arrived, looking a little wide-eyed and

pale, they were all set to pour drinks ready for the guests, before Taylor disappeared into her office.

Kayleigh watched Ben serve the guests, laughing and joking with them, but every time he met her stare, his eyes shuttered. What the hell was going on?

They took a break while Taylor gave a heart-felt speech about love, toasting the happy couple before everyone poured over to the bar. Then they were back working in sync, moving swiftly past each other but now, Ben no longer gripped her by the waist, no longer brushed against her. In fact, he actively avoided her, and she was beginning to feel pissed. She didn't understand. Was he feeling weird about what she said to him?

Later, as the evening was winding down, Kayleigh glimpsed Taylor talking to Sheriff Blake and his fiancé Justine, then Beau came over and wrapped his arms around Taylor. When they kissed, Kayleigh grinned and happiness, only happiness, flooded her that the two of them had made up.

Christy, the bride and Taylor's best friend, broke away from her new husband and came over to the bar, needing some water.

"Can I just say you look absolutely stunning, Christy, congratulations!" Kayleigh enthused. The petite blond flushed prettily, and Kayleigh pushed a pint of water across the bar to her.

"Thank you, darlin', that's very sweet of you," she replied, gulping the water down.

"Do you feel any different to before you married?"

"I don't know, not yet I don't think. Ask me in a few years." Christy's eyes drifted back to Dean who was now dancing with Taylor, his stepsister, and Christy chuckled. "Is it weird and unfeminist of me to say I feel like my life didn't truly start until that man blundered his way back

Love Me Good

into it?"

"Not at all, it's the people we meet that make our lives what they are. He's your husband, you're kinda stuck with him now."

"Yeah, I guess I am," she replied, a soft smile playing at her lips as she watched him. "Thanks Kayleigh. Have you got anyone in your life?"

She darted a look at Ben. "I'm not sure."

"That sounds like a yes to me. I was in the same boat once and look at me now."

"How did you do it?"

"I honestly don't know, sorry. I thought I would be good at giving sage relationship advice, but I think I've had too much champagne. If you need other life advice, then maybe I can help?"

This was her moment, Kayleigh could feel it. To kickstart a journey to cross off the number one task on her list: start her writing career. She'd been so scared that her research would tell her that what she wanted was impossible so she had put it off for as long as she could.

"Actually…" she began then stopped herself. *It's Christy's wedding day for God's sake, she doesn't need this right now.* "Never mind."

"Kayleigh," Christy warned. "Out with it."

"It's your wedding day, I can't!" she hissed.

Christy laughed again. "As long as it's not my wedding *night*, we're good, darlin'. What's on your mind?"

Kayleigh tugged at the corner of her white blouse and nibbled her lip. She felt bad hitting Christy up for advice and help on her special day, but this could be the last time she would get the nerve to do it.

"I was after some writing advice, please, if that's okay?"

Christy's eyes immediately lit up. "Oh my God, for

real? You're a writer too?"

"Well, kinda? Not really."

"You are, accept it. What is it you write?"

"I like to write the storylines for games." She held her breath, waiting for Christy to laugh in her face, but she didn't.

"That's so exciting. How many have you written?"

Kayleigh squirmed. "A dozen or so."

"Kayleigh!" Christy squealed. "That's amazing! Have you sent them off to anyone?"

"Well, that's it, I don't really know what to do. I want to do this as a career and it's my passion, but I don't know if I'm any good. How do I even do this? Coming from little old Citrus Pines, who would take me seriously? What if I failed? What if…"

Christy cut her off. "What if you're amazing and get everything you ever dreamed of?"

Kayleigh rolled her lips inwards. "Then there's that…"

"It sounds to me like you have imposter syndrome. Tell it to fuck off, right this second. It will cripple you from doing anything. Do you want me to take a look at some of your stuff?"

"I couldn't ask you to do that!"

"You didn't, I offered. Look here's my email address, send it to me and I'll read it and give you some feedback." She took the pen from Kayleigh's blouse pocket and scribbled her details on a cocktail napkin before sliding it across to the bar with a wink. "But Kayleigh, hear me loud and clear, you *can* do this. It doesn't matter that you come from a small town, it doesn't matter that no one knows you. Make them know you." Christy added, fierceness dripping from her words. "Trust me."

Then she flounced away back to her husband, with

Kayleigh calling weakly after her, "Thank you!"

Out the corner of her eye she saw Ben heading down the corridor towards the restrooms and kitchen. She hurried after him, eager to share the news of how she'd garnered her courage, taken a chance, and it had paid off.

"Ben!" she hissed, following his retreating back. He stopped and turned towards her, a frown puckering his forehead, and her thumb twitched with the need to reach up and smooth it away.

"Yeah?"

"I did it!" she squealed.

"Did what?"

She did a little wiggle of her hips. "I took a chance."

He cleared his throat. "Oh yeah?"

"I asked Christy to read my story. Well, she insisted actually, but I'm going to send it to her, and she's going to read it and let me have her thoughts."

"That's incredible!" he whooped and threw his arms around her. She laughed as he enveloped her, his scent invading her nostrils and she buried her face in his chest.

"I'm so proud of you, Kay," he said, his palm smoothing a line down her spine and making her shiver.

"Kay. You've never called me Kay before," she murmured, thinking of her online friend with kind-of benefits.

"Uh, new nickname, it just felt right."

She pulled away and looked into his face, beaming down at hers and any awkwardness that she felt earlier washed away.

"That's my girl," he said, pride and heat tearing through her at his words. Then he lifted his hand and trailed a finger down the slope of her nose, slowly, their eyes connected the entire time, his promising her things she couldn't name. She sucked in a breath, the sound ruining the moment and he broke the spell by booping the tip of her nose. *Friend zoned.*

"Thanks, I uh, just wanted to share that with you."

"I'm glad," he replied. And then suddenly that awkwardness settled over them again. She hated it, it had never existed until today and she didn't know why. She opened her mouth to ask him, but he spoke first.

"I'd better get back out there, lots of thirsty wedding guests waiting." He rocked forward on the balls of his feet, his hands shoved deep into the pockets of his dress pants before he swiveled and disappeared.

*

Ben turned away from her, shutting out the excitement and triumph in her eyes that sparkled at him so invitingly and the smile that was so bright it was as though it had stripped the neon from all the lights. If he didn't leave now, then he was liable to shove her against the nearest wall and reward her for being so brave and confident.

He had tried to avoid her all day, feeling like an asshole for what happened between them online last night. He had taken things way too far, but she was getting under his skin like no one else had, carving her way through his veins and heading directly for his heart.

He knew he was half in love with her when he took the risk of moving here, but now? Now she was pretty much settled there for all eternity. Only he was stuck in this weird limbo of being her close friend online and her friend in real life where they had kinda, sorta shared a super-hot kiss and he didn't know where to go from there. *To the bedroom would be my advice*, his dick piped up. But that was the problem last night, being around Kayleigh all evening had him all riled up. He hadn't been thinking with the right piece of his anatomy and he had potentially ruined everything between them. He shouldn't have sent those messages. It was wrong and he was muddying the water of any potential future they had.

He had been so nervous to see her today, hating that she didn't know she was talking to him online, and that was another asshole move on his part. He wanted to tell her the truth, but he also didn't want to change the path they were on in real life. He was just an asshole all round right now. And this asshole needed to get away from her fast before he took things even further.

He headed back down the corridor, away from her. He could see customers, wedding guests, the bridal party, for fuck's sake, he was so close to getting away from her.

And then suddenly, he wasn't.

"Ben, wait," she said, gripping his arm and that was all it took. Her dainty fingers, wrapping around the flesh of his forearm. Then she was pressed against the wall, his pelvis pinning her in place, his mouth crushing to hers, capturing the surprised moan that quickly turned erotic beneath the sweep of his tongue. His hand tangled in her hair, tugging slightly to change the angle, to sink deeper. Her hands gripped his shoulder, her fingers digging in and holding on as he worked her over.

His little bad girl.

Laughter from the bar pulled him from the depths of his desire, reminding him where they were.

He broke the kiss. "Come with me," he whispered urgently. She nodded and he grasped her hand, pulling her through the kitchen and out the back door, around the side of the building. She rounded on him, shoving him against the wall, his cock swelling further against the seam of his pants at her aggression. He gripped her thighs beneath her little black skirt that had teased him all damn day, sliding up and around to the curve of her ass, his fingers spreading wide to cover her cheeks.

"Finally," she murmured, her sweet breath fanning his face. Her arms ran up his torso and latched around his neck. She slid her tongue across his bottom lip and he huffed out a breath then buried his face, trailing kisses up her neck, sucking hard, determined to put his mark on her.

His fingers found the way to the front of her blouse, shaking and fumbling with need as he tried to unbutton it, pulling the blouse to one side. A guttural noise left his throat as her delicate hand palmed his cock, squeezing tightly.

He pulled her bra to the side and dipped his head taking her pretty pink nipple into his mouth and her fingers dove through his hair, tugging sharply. His tongue flicked back and forth, fast and she rubbed herself against his crotch. He pulled his mouth away with a *pop* and nipped the skin around her breast then moved to her other nipple, his fingers playing with its damp twin.

"Oh *shit*," she groaned. The curse from her sweet lips had him thrusting up into her and sucking harder. He left her breast as she fumbled at his shirt, unbuttoning and then her hands were on his chest, nails digging in as she gripped him tight.

His mouth crashed to hers, their tongues warring as they both panted for breath. She nibbled and sucked and moaned her way through the kiss and he decided this kiss was going in his memory Hall of Fame. Nothing would ever knock this off the top spot. He slid his hands around and cupped her ass again, squeezing tightly and crushing her to him, rubbing her back and forth over his aching length.

"Touch me, please," she breathed into his ear. He

found the crotch of her panties, already damp with her desire and rubbed his knuckle over the center. Her breath hitched and he swallowed her moan.

"Does that feel good, Kayleigh?"

"You know it does," she growled, and he chuckled at the beast he'd awaken in the town's sweetheart. "Harder, Ben."

Her command and his name from her lips had him slipping his hand under the edge of her panties and into her wet heat. He slid two fingers inside her and his eyes rolled back in his head as she clenched around him, desperate to keep him in paradise. When she relaxed her muscles, he spread his fingers wide and thrust them in and out.

"Is that better?"

"Mmm…"

"Say my name, Kay." He needed to hear it, needed to know that she wasn't off in a fantasy thinking of someone else. Needed to know that she was as desperate for him as he was for her. That she was falling with no safety net, just like he was.

"Ben," she sighed and bucked her hips, pumping herself up and down on him. His tongue slid out and over her nipple, torturing the hard point while she worked herself on his hands, her breaths and cries getting higher and he couldn't wait to watch her fall.

"Ben, I'm going to…"

A throat cleared in their vicinity and Kayleigh pulled back gasping. Ben threw himself in front of her, acting like a human shield as the deputy sheriff appeared from around the side of the building.

"I'm not sure what Taylor's paying you for, but I don't think it's this," Blake said, his voice stern but there was an undercurrent of humor there too, not that his expression betrayed it. Blake tried to peer around Ben which sent all Ben's alpha instincts soaring, his adrenaline riding him hard. Blake noticed the change in him and didn't appreciate it one bit.

"You can take it down a notch son, I'm the sheriff and you're in a public place. I could arrest you both for what you were just doing. I'm not going to, so maybe tell your face that."

Ben tried to get his anger under control. Blake was a good guy and Ben knew that he had a point.

"Appreciate that, sir," Ben said, his voice gruff.

"Good, now y'all have a good evening," Blake said and sauntered back around the side of the bar. Ben turned back to Kayleigh, helping her right her clothing before tugging her back towards the bar.

"Are we in trouble?" Her face twisted with concern. As much as she tried to pretend she was a rebel, the real Kayleigh was still as sweet, good and considerate as ever.

"No Kay, we're not."

"He's not gonna tell my parents that he caught us doing that, is he?"

Ben would have laughed if he didn't realize how anxious she was. He never wanted to do anything that would compromise her, she was his best friend, the best person in his life, not that she knew it. "No Kay, you're twenty-six. He won't tell your parents anything."

Her relief was palpable. "Good."

They went back to work like nothing happened, but Ben didn't know what to say, how to feel. Who knows how far they would have gone outside if they hadn't been caught. What if they'd gone even further and been caught then and she would be mortified, people would talk, and they wouldn't look at her the same way. He didn't want to be that person who knocked her off her pedestal, he only wanted to lift her up.

When he got home that night, he logged onto his computer and sat waiting for her, with Geralt in his lap, nibbling some kale. When that tell-tale noise echoed throughout his room, he didn't waste any time.

GreenEyedKing96: I'm so sorry.
GoodGirlKay: For what?
GreenEyedKing96: For what I did yesterday, I took things to a place where we haven't been before without your consent and I'm sorry.
GoodGirlKay: Without my consent? You saw me replying right?
GreenEyedKing96: You know what I mean. We had never spoken like…that…before and I didn't discuss with you if that was a direction you wanted us to move in.
GoodGirlKay: Well, what if it is?

Ben didn't know how to feel about that. Did she want a physical or 'touch ourselves while we chat' kind of relationship with him online whilst unknowingly continuing a physical relationship with him offline? He felt weirdly jealous of himself. But Kayleigh didn't know he was both Ben and GreenEyedKing96. He wanted to pursue things with her in person so he had to shut this down, no matter how painful the consequences could be.

GreenEyedKing96: I don't think we should, I think I'm kind of seeing someone and it wouldn't be right to do that with you, again.
GoodGirlKay is typing…
Pause.
GoodGirlKay is typing…
Pause.

GreenEyedKing96: Our friendship is too important to me, I hope I haven't ruined anything.
GoodGirlKay is typing...
Pause.
GoodGirlKay: What do you say when you lose a Nintendo game?

The knot in Ben's chest eased and he smiled, big and wide for all to see, well, for Geralt to see. They would be okay, she was taking them back to old, familiar territory and he was beyond grateful. *I do not deserve her.*

GreenEyedKing96: I've missed these. I don't know...
GoodGirlKay: I want a wii-match!

Ben's laugh echoed around his room so loud that he startled Geralt who bounced into the air before landing solidly in Ben's lap again, giving him a nibble of discontent. Ben ruffled his fur in apology, but the smile stayed on his lips. Now he had fixed things with her online, he just needed to work out how to progress with her in real life.

GreenEyedKing96: #perfection
GoodGirlKay: Also I have some news regarding my stories...
GreenEyedKing96: Tell me all about it, Kay xx

*

Chapter 11

He messaged Kayleigh the next day, eager to see her again.

Ben: Any plans for your evening off?

He wondered if she would have second thoughts about getting to know him after being caught getting busy by the sheriff. Maybe she didn't want to hang around with someone who could get her arrested in the blink of an eye like he could.

His phone vibrated and he glanced down, eager to see her reply but instead there was a message from his brother.

Matt: Are you alive?

Seeing his brother's name immediately brought back visions of his family's laughing faces, mocking him and his career choice. Nausea churned Ben's stomach. Matt's words immediately prickled his anger. He could almost hear the disdain in his brother's words, practically envisage the bored expression on his face. He wasn't going to reply. Not now, not ever.

Matt: I mean it, I'm worried. At least let Mom know you're okay.

His anger increased because he realized Matt was right. He should at least let her know he was okay. But he knew if he messaged her there would just be more responses, more questions. Despite his thoughts from just moments before, he replied.

Ben: Alive.

That should keep them quiet, and he knew his brother would pass the information along to their mom. Two seconds later his phone vibrated again and he picked it up, ready to block Matt's number, but saw it was Kayleigh.

Kayleigh: I was thinking of heading to the next county and causing some trouble, might start a ruckus or maybe I'll just stay home and read a book instead. Sometimes rebelling is exhausting.

He smiled. He loved that she tried to push herself to rebel, because frankly, she wasn't that good at it. She was too sweet still, too gentle and she cared way too much what other people thought of her. She tried, but Kayleigh 2.0 was still a big ol' softy.

Ben: Well if you manage to rest up I was thinking we could hang out? There's somewhere else I wanted to show you.

Ben had done some research after their night hanging out at the bar, when they had their first kiss. He wanted to help her and knew what she needed: confidence. She was the only one who could get it, but she just needed a little push.

Kayleigh: I guess I could pry myself away…what did you have in mind?

He grinned while tapping out his reply.

Ben: I'll pick you up at 6:30, wear something athletic.

That evening, he pulled up outside her house. While he waited for her to come out, he spotted the curtain twitch and a woman's face appeared in the window. He lifted his hand and waved at her mom. Kayleigh's mom looked startled at being spotted but lifted her arm and returned his wave.
Kayleigh came out the front door and ran towards his car wearing black yoga pants and a light blue tank top, her peach hair fluttering around her shoulders.
"Busy day rebelling?" he asked when she opened the car door.
"Very, but luckily for you I found some energy." She winked at him, and his heart tugged in his chest. She looked so adorable.

"Where are we going?"

He started the car and pulled away from the curb. "You'll have to see."

Out the corner of his eye he saw her pull her lip between her teeth, nibbling on it and he was glad his hands were already occupied, so he couldn't reach across and grab her. As they drove, he asked her to tell him about the story she was working on. She hesitated at first and then it burst out of her. Although he already knew what her story was about, the way she told it and seeing her passion face to face had him spellbound. He was almost sad when they reached their destination.

He reluctantly pulled the car over. "We're here."

She looked around her at the street. "Where's here?"

He reached across and tilted her chin up. When she spotted the neon sign, *Intrigue*, he heard her swallow.

"I, uh, did some digging. Get your cute butt in there and work that pole," he said. When she didn't move, he panicked. "This is the place, right? From the flier you described? I went looking for it and found this place but maybe it's the wrong one."

She shook her head before facing him, her expression earnest. "It's the right one. How did you…why are you helping me so much?"

He shrugged. "I like seeing my friends become the people they want to be. I want to encourage them to be their best versions of themselves."

"So, friends then. This definitely isn't a date?"

He looked at her, her hands wringing in her lap, her teeth sinking into her soft bottom lip. He turned his body, taking up the space between them and her eyelids dipped. The air around him changed and he struggled for breath, like fire starved of oxygen.

"It can be a date if you want it to be a date?" Silence

filled the car. "Is that what you want, Kayleigh?" he added. He wanted to push her to use her words. To speak up for what she wanted, like she had at the bar that night.

"Yes," she breathed.

"Good, then I'm glad we're on the same page. Now get in there and go find out just how sexy you really are," he murmured. Her wide eyes left his, flicking to look through the car window at the building. She swallowed again and he saw her tremor, but he wasn't sure whether it was from fear or excitement.

"I'll be waiting for you when you're done, I want to hear all about it." He leaned forward and pressed a kiss to the corner of her mouth, then opened her door and unclicked her seatbelt.

She paused before getting out of the car slowly, like she was trying to find the courage to do it.

"I believe in you. You can do this, I swear," he said. She met his eyes, hers glittering before her expression hardened and she slammed the car door shut. He watched her walk towards the building, her steps becoming more sure the closer she got until she had her hand on the door. She shot him another look over her shoulder, a triumphant smile on her face and he let out a laugh. With that she waltzed inside.

He shook his head smiling, how did she do it? Screw *'be more E.P'*, *'be more Kayleigh'* should be his new motto. She amazed him, she inspired him. Watching her go for what she wanted and pushing her boundaries had inspired him. He knew something was missing in his life. Ever since she had talked about that adrenaline rush she felt at the waterfall, it had been nagging at him, and it was only watching her go for what she wanted that he recognized what he was doing.

He had let the thoughts and opinions of those close to

him affect how he felt about the one thing he was truly passionate about. Everyone wanted their family members to accept them for who they are and what they do, but that just wasn't possible with his family because they valued different things in life. Their actions had made him shy away from performing, had made him quit altogether. But should he care what they thought? The one person he'd loved most, his grandma, had been his biggest supporter. What was he doing, turning his back on his passion?

He turned the car around. He needed to be back for Kayleigh in an hour, which meant he had the perfect amount of time. He drove back towards Citrus Pines, through the town and out towards The Rusty Bucket Inn. He parked up at the lot and hurried inside, excitement driving him forward, and made a beeline for Taylor.

"Hey, you're not supposed to be working today!" the redhead scolded when she saw him.

He pulled her to the side. "I need a favor, can we talk?"

*

Come on feet, work!

Kayleigh stared up at the building, that bright neon sign that was beckoning to her, willing herself to find the confidence to go inside.

"I believe in you. You can do this, I swear," Ben called to her. She turned to meet his eyes and something in them spurred her on. She could do this. He believed in her, he just *knew* she could do it.

Resolve fused her spine, pushing her feet forward, one in front of the other until she felt Kayleigh 2.0 take over. One hand on the door, she shot him a smile that said *you're right, I can do this,* and then she went inside.

The studio was split into two halves with metal poles reaching floor to ceiling. Some women were already wrapping themselves around them, contorting into impossible shapes and Kayleigh watched with awe. Low music pumped out and the lights dimmed. Other women sat on the polished wooden floor, their legs spread in deep stretches.

"Hi, welcome to *Intrigue*. Is this your first time?" A woman appeared next to her. Kayleigh tore her eyes away from another who was spinning around and around on the pole, lowering herself towards the ground.

"Yes," Kayleigh replied, then faced the woman. She looked to be in her mid-forties, her copper hair pulled back into a high ponytail, some threads of silver shining in the light. Freckles scattered across her nose but left her cheeks clear. She wore large silver earrings, a chunky necklace and a black tank top with black short shorts.

"Have you ever done any pole work before?" the woman asked.

Kayleigh shook her head.

"A true beginner, so exciting!" the woman squealed and gestured for Kayleigh to follow her. She took her bag and asked Kayleigh to remove her shoes and socks.

"I'm Sandi and this is my business. I have two rules: no pro moves until I say you're ready and no comparing yourself to others in the class. I'll teach you the basics. Do not try and run before you can walk as that's how people get hurt. What's your name, hon?"

"Kayleigh."

"And what drew you here in the first place?"

Kayleigh looked around at the other women. Some just trying to pull themselves up the pole and struggling, some in complicated poses, some swaying their bodies sensually to the music. There were definitely different levels of experience here and she felt less intimidated at seeing the beginners.

"I want to do something different, something exciting. I want to be sexy, to feel strong and capable," she explained.

Sandi smiled at her and nodded. "Then it sounds like you came to the right place, come with me."

She looped her arm through Kayleigh's and took her over to one of the free poles and stood Kayleigh next to it, facing the wall of mirrors in front of her.

"I want you to take a look at the girl in front of you. She *is* strong, she *is* powerful and capable, she *is* sexy. Now we've just got to convince her and we're gonna do that together, hon." Sandi squeezed her arm briefly before turning and speaking to one of the other girls who had come over. If she hadn't done that, she might have noticed the quiver in Kayleigh's lip or the way she cleared her throat and took a breath, suddenly overcome with emotion.

By the time Sandi turned back, Kayleigh had a big smile plastered on her face.

"Now then, let's stretch out and we'll start with the basics…"

*

When Ben pulled up outside the studio, Kayleigh rushed over, opened the car door and threw herself inside peppering kisses over his face.

"Thank you so much for pushing me to do this, it was amazing," she said in between kisses.

He laughed and gripped her arms. "I'm so pleased, you going back next week?" She nodded eagerly and he laughed again. "That's my bad girl, I'm so proud of you."

Then he pulled her close for a kiss, covering her lips with his before teasing them open and driving her wild with smooth wet strokes of his tongue. She pressed herself against him, needing to be closer. A low sound rose in his throat that made her needy, clutching at the sleeves of his leather jacket and tugging him impossibly closer.

"Dammit, Kay. I need to get you out of here before something indecent happens in the middle of this crowded street."

She glanced around, seeing no one nearby, and giggled. He pulled himself away, groaning, just as her stomach let out a loud growl. She clapped her hand over her belly, heat fusing her cheeks.

"Looks like I need to feed you first. Ruby's okay?"

"We can go and do something else if you like? If you're bored?"

He scoffed. "How can I be bored? There's nothing more exciting than being with you."

Warmth spread through her. She looked at him, taking in his brilliant green eyes, his dirty blond hair swept back, his leather jacket. He looked like some kind of fifties rock star and he wanted to take *her* for dinner? He wanted them to be more than friends? Hell yes, please and thank you, ma'am.

He gripped her hand and linked their fingers together, resting them on his knee as he drove and she launched into a rapid explanation of meeting Sandi, her excitement carrying her words away. She told him about the techniques Sandi had shown her and what some of the other women were doing and the timeline which Kayleigh expected to achieve them by.

When they arrived at the diner, he held the door open

for her as they entered. She loved this place and the enigmatic owner who greeted them.

"Well now, ain't you a pretty looking couple?" Ruby crowed, sizing them up and down. "I think he would look better with me but on this occasion, I'll adhere to girl code and step aside for you, sweet cheeks."

Kayleigh laughed. "Thank you, Ruby. It's a great sacrifice, I know."

Ruby waved them into a booth, her eyes lingering on Ben, and Kayleigh began to think she would launch herself at him. Hell, she couldn't blame the woman, he was gorgeous. He just had something—an aura—about him.

Once they ordered their food, Ben took her palm in his, his thumb rubbing small circles against her skin and she sighed, truly happy.

"Can you tell me about your family and your life before you moved here?"

"Why do you wanna know about that?" he asked, rubbing the back of his neck with his free hand.

"Because I want to get to know you, you're a mystery. Also, it's a massive red flag if you don't want to share about your past," Kayleigh replied.

"I just don't like talking about it, that's all."

"Massive walking red flag."

He snorted. "It's boring."

"I'll be the judge of that," she said and removed her palm from his, playing hardball. She folded her hands together and gazed at him with interest. She was in listening mode.

He sighed and began playing with the cutlery on the table. "We don't get along. We're not cut from the same kind of cloth."

When Kayleigh didn't say more, using silence to see

how he would react, he continued.

"They're business and academic focused. There was a lot of pressure to follow in my father's footsteps and become the next in line to inherit the clinic. My brother has done a stellar job, my father has an heir in all the ways he wanted one. But I just never...fit. I was never good enough for them. They looked down on me, belittled me. My father is a well-known surgeon, famous actually. My brother just qualified, and is set to follow right in my father's footsteps. Everyone is overflowing with pride, and I'm just...a failure."

Kayleigh's heart ached at seeing how much he was beating himself up for being different. There was nothing wrong with different. Different was interesting.

"You're not a failure, what makes you think that?"

He shrugged. "I tried. I really tried to do what they wanted but I'm just not wired that way."

"You said before you had medical training?"

"I tried to become a paramedic. But even that wasn't good enough, why would I be a 'lowly paramedic' when I could have been a world-renowned surgeon like my dad? They looked down on me for not living up to their legacy."

She reached across the table and took his hands in hers and gave them a squeeze, hating what his family had done to him, what they had put him through, making him doubt himself so strongly.

"I'm intrigued to hear what kind of cloth you are cut from then if you don't want that kind of career?"

He tugged at the collar of his shirt and wouldn't meet her eyes. "Well, I guess I like music and perf-"

They were interrupted by Ruby bringing their food over, flirting some more with Ben and entertaining them with her raunchy humor. The old woman definitely had a soft spot for him, again, who could blame her?

"Where were we? Oh wait, I was wondering if something in particular made you move here?" she asked when Ruby left them.

Ben winced. "One night, I discovered my girlfriend had been seeing my brother behind my back. Not only that but she also told him some…sensitive information which he chose to share with the family during a private event and well, they humiliated me. That on top of everything just…I had to get away, I had to leave, Kay." He met her eyes with a desperation that made her want to wrap him in her arms and never let go.

"I'm sorry they did that to you. Families should never betray each other like that, and your brother and your ex-girlfriend sound pretty sucky to me."

He smiled gently at her words.

"Do you miss them?" she asked softly.

He pursed his lips, his expression confused, like he wasn't sure or not.

"Either way, I'm sorry for what happened to you, no one deserves that. And although I would have *words* if I ever saw them, I'm glad you came here, and we got to meet."

He smiled at her, full force, the pain briefly forgotten.

"So, what games do you play?"

His eyes lit up. "I didn't mention it before, but I also play Queen's Ransom."

"You do? How did you get past the Lunatic Jester? I've been struggling with that for ages!"

"Ah, I don't think I'm at that point yet, I've only just found the Potion of Light," he replied.

"Ugh, that took me ages. I couldn't work it out until I talked it through with a friend who figured out that you just have to bribe the-"

"Howling Monkeys with the enchanted bananas?"

"Yes!" she shook her head, amazed. "You knew that too? I could not figure it out for the life of me."

He shrugged, a small smile playing around his lips and a look in his eye that she hadn't seen before; they were bright like wildfire, burning her all over with their scorching intensity.

"So, it's Thanksgiving in two weeks. I know we've only known each other for over a month but would you maybe wanna spend it with me and my parents?" she asked, worried he would refuse or that he would think she was taking things too fast, but instead he nodded.

"I would love nothing more."

Ben drove her home, holding her hand the entire way before pressing a soft kiss to her lips, trailing along her jaw and finishing at the tender spot just behind her ear.

"See you tomorrow, bad girl."

Lord, when he called her that she wanted to be bad, but only for him.

*

Chapter 12

"I'll get it!" Kayleigh yelled when the doorbell rang. Excitement drove her steps towards the door, she was so eager to see him. She threw it open and there he was, looking festive in a burgundy and rust patterned sweatshirt, his blue jeans turned up at the ankles showing off his tan boots. He wrapped an arm around her waist, pulling her close and she went, fitting to him perfectly.

"You look beautiful," he murmured in her ear, pressing a kiss to the shell, his breath warming it had goosebumps raising all over her skin.

"And who is this handsome young man?" Kayleigh pulled away when her mother appeared.

"Hi, I'm Ben, lovely to meet you, Mrs. Good. These are for you, ma'am," he said, holding out some white roses that Kayleigh only just noticed and dang if her heart didn't flutter at the gesture, or the way he *ma'am*'ed her mom.

"Lovely to meet you, Ben. Please, call me Maureen." Kayleigh watched her mom take the flowers, positive that she was blushing. "Albert, come meet Kayleigh's young man!" Maureen called before heading back into the kitchen.

"I'm sorry, I haven't told her we're not official or anything. She didn't mean you were *my* young man," Kayleigh whispered.

Ben turned towards her, his mouth quirked up on one side. "I'm not?"

"Do you want to be?" left her mouth before she could stop it.

"More than anything."

The fire in his eyes had her pulse pounding hard, her throat tightening and the urge to drag him up to her room would have overtaken her, if her father hadn't appeared.

"Hello Ben, pleased to meet you. I'm Albert," he said, sticking his hand out. Her dad believed a man who was worth his salt had a firm handshake but didn't try to intimidate the person whose hand he was shaking. Kayleigh watched as Ben gripped her father's hand and shook once, twice and she held her breath as she looked to her dad for his verdict. Albert smiled and nodded at Kayleigh and her breath released in a quiet *whoosh*. Proud of Ben for passing a test he didn't know he had just faced, she fetched him a drink and returned to the living room to find him and her father chatting.

"Kayleigh tells me you like blues music?"

Ben sat forward in his seat. "Yeah, and Motown. Not traditional for someone my age but I spent a lot of time with my grandma when I was a kid. She was always playing it and I just loved it. I have great memories of the two of us going through her old records. When she passed, she left them all to me."

"I'm sorry to hear she passed, she sounds like a great lady with good taste."

Kayleigh watched as Ben seemed to disappear into a memory and her heart ached for his loss. He had mentioned his grandma a few times in the last couple of weeks, but she hadn't realized just how close they had been.

He came back to himself a moment later, fixing his gaze back on her father. "What about you?"

"I'm a blues and soul man myself. Love me some B.B King, Etta James and of course, Elvis. You like Elvis?" Albert said, focusing on Ben.

Ben began to rub his palms over his thighs. "Yeah of course, I mean, who doesn't like Elvis?"

Her father nodded, a reminiscent smile on his lips. "You know, you kinda remind me of him. I met him once when I was a kid."

A garbled sound left Ben, and Kayleigh fixed him with a strange look as he cleared his throat.

"What was he like?" Awe dripped from Ben's tone and Kayleigh watched as he leaned even closer, getting drawn into the conversation. Her father began describing every moment of meeting Elvis. He had only been eight so Kayleigh was surprised he could remember so much but he always said, *You never forget meeting a man like that.* Looking over at Ben, taking in the shape of his body, the curves that made up his face and reflecting on the way he made her feel, she had a vague idea of what her father meant.

She watched as Ben stared at her father, drinking in every detail, every crumb her father gave him with rapt fascination. A thrill shot through her at how well they were getting on and she was almost disappointed when her mom called them all to dinner.

She and Ben sat next to each other at the table, and she tried to keep the smile off her face when he pressed his thigh to hers, keeping them connected. When they went around the table and stated what they were thankful for, a lump formed in her throat when Ben announced, loud and proud, "I'm thankful for meeting your wonderful daughter, Kayleigh. So incredibly thankful."

"Oh, Albert," her mom sighed, gripping her father's hand.

"That's a good answer, son," her father replied gruffly.

*

"I wanna see your computer…" Ben whispered in her ear when her parents weren't looking.

"Oh yeah?" she murmured, a sly look in her eye that drove Ben wild.

"Yeah, then I'll show you my hard drive." He waggled his eyebrows, and she cupped a hand over her mouth, muffling a snort.

"Lame jokes are my thing!" she hissed.

"I know," he replied and then her brows dipped in and she stared at him. He realized his goof, she hadn't done 'lame' jokes with *Ben*, she'd done them with GreenEyedKing96.

He took her hand, trying to distract himself from his guilt. "Come on."

She threw a glance over her shoulder and saw her parents lost in conversation in the kitchen. When she turned back to him that smirk lifted her lips again and he knew he was in trouble.

She giggled as she dragged him up the stairs and into

her room, closing the door softly before she turned to face him. He glanced around her room, taking in the patterned wallpaper in soft gentle tones and warm colored furnishings. The room felt like home, it felt like *her*.

His gaze landed on her computer. White monitor with a light pink keyboard and mouse, multicolored lights flashing from the base unit underneath, and he just knew if he typed on the keyboard it would light up.

To see the place where she sat nearly every night talking to him, where they exchanged so many messages, so many jokes, deep conversations and so much love, not that she knew it, did something funny to his insides.

"Wanna know my hard drive capacity?" she spoke softly as she stared at him.

"Not right now," he grunted and whirled around, lifting her off her feet and burying his face in her neck, needing to breathe her in. To assure himself that she was real, that he was really here, with her.

He peppered kisses over her satin skin, loving the hitch in her breath as his tongue slid up the side of her neck. He backed her towards the bed and dropped down, landing softly on top of her as his lips swept over hers, his hand tangling in her pale peach hair.

"I believe I owe you an orgasm."

"Ben," she moaned, a sweet sound from her sweet lips. He would never get enough of her. He felt her tense beneath him as someone coughed from outside her room on the landing.

"I've never had a man in my room before," she whispered. He pulled back, staring down at her mouth and her flushed cheeks, her shining eyes.

"Have you had a woman in here before?"

"Nope, no one."

"Dang, so no magic has happened here? I'm the first?" He couldn't explain why that made him as thrilled as it did.

"Only magic I've created myself," she replied with a quirk of her brow.

He groaned. "You're killing me, bad girl. Alone or with assistance?"

Her cheeks flushed deeper at his question, and he watched as she tried to fight back a small smile.

"Kayleigh Good, are you blushing?"

"No," she said and immediately tried to hide her face in his neck.

He chuckled. "Judging by that reaction you definitely have *assistance*. Where do you keep it?"

"I'm not telling you!" she gasped, then clapped a hand over her mouth to keep the noise down.

"Why?" he purred in her ear, and she shifted underneath him restlessly. "I'll make you *so glad* you did," he added, lacing his tone with as much promise as possible. Her eyes widened ever so slightly; he wouldn't have noticed if he wasn't already so close to her. He gently thrust his hips into her, watching her reaction and wishing it was his lip she was nibbling rather than her own. She groaned and covered her face with one hand while pointing to her bedside drawers with the other and triumph flickered through him.

He leaned to the side, his arm reaching across and pulling open the drawer. He rifled around inside until his hand landed on what he was looking for. He hit her with what he hoped was a wicked smile, a devilish smile.

He drew out the purple silicone vibrator and arched a brow at her when he took in the size. Kayleigh worried that bottom lip again. "You're not gonna compare yourself to that right? There's nothing to worry about."

"Are you kidding me? Me and this guy are a lil team now, in charge of one thing only," he said, flicking the switch and it started gently buzzing in his palm. He'd never held one before and just stared at the contraption for a moment.

"Oh my God, I can't believe you're holding that," Kayleigh groaned, clapping her hands over her eyes.

He chuckled again. "Believe it, things are about to be a whole lot of fun." He sat up slightly, pressing a quick kiss to her lips, nipping her chin before flipping up the edge of her navy dress. He took in her floral panties with a little frilly trim and decided they were perfect for Kayleigh. He ran his fingers through the silky edging and she giggled when he tickled her skin.

He lifted his eyes to meet hers and the blue depths consumed him. He ran the vibrator over her thighs, tickling her and she started squirming as he raised it higher, until he pressed gently over her center. She arched her back, rolled her hips into it and his eyes drank in the sight of her. He pressed more firmly and a soft moan slipped from her lips before she clamped a hand over her mouth and looked at him, her expression horrified.

"Oh God, my parents are downstairs!"

"Then I guess you'd better keep it down, bad girl." He tugged her panties down and pressed a kiss to her lower belly, over her hip before he dipped lower and slid his tongue through her wet center. She tasted as sweet as she looked, with a hint of sin. She rocked her hips up to meet him as he swiped his tongue over her again. She grabbed the nearest pillow and pulled it over her mouth to muffle her response. He licked again before nudging her thighs wider apart with his shoulders and then brought his new acquaintance into the game.

He rubbed the vibrator back and forth over her clit

and watched her entire body tense. Her hands reached out to grab onto something and tangled in the quilt covers. He drew the toy down further to her entrance and slowly pushed it inside. A strangled gasp came from underneath the pillow and if it wasn't so sexy he would have been laughing at how much she was trying to control herself. As it was, he wanted her to completely fall apart right in front of his eyes. He *needed* this.

Ben thrust the vibrator in and out slowly and bent his head to lick and suck at her clit. He hummed and the added vibrations traveled through her body. Her knees squeezed either side of his head and he reveled in the exquisite pain his pleasure was bringing her.

Her breath left her in pants as with each flick of his tongue her hips rose up to meet him until she was tensing, clamping her muscles down around the toy and a strangled cry emanated from above his head. Her body went limp, completely boneless and he gently removed the toy and pulled the pillow away.

Her eyes were bright, but her lids lowered and she offered him a sleepy smile.

"That was…"

"I'd like to take full credit but…" he trailed off and gestured to the vibrator.

She giggled, taking it from him and pressed a delicate kiss to his lips. "I'll be back and you better be ready when I am," she murmured.

When she left the room his phone buzzed in his back pocket, it had been going off the whole time he was there but he had ignored it. He pulled it out and saw it was his brother trying to call him. Ben let it go to voicemail before he unlocked his phone and scrolled through the messages.

There was one after the other from Matt, asking Ben

where he was, why he wasn't answering and lots of words he couldn't make out. Was he drunk? This was out of character for stoic Matt and something niggled at Ben. His brother rang again just as Kayleigh reappeared. She slid her arms around him from behind and nestled herself against his back. The affection from her was what he loved the most, some guys weren't all hugs and kisses and hand holding but Ben loved it. *Touch me all the time, affection is my love language.*

He was eager to continue his evening with Kayleigh but now he was worried about Matt.

"I'm really sorry Kay, but I've gotta go. Something's going on and I'm not sure what," he said, lifting his phone.

Her face shuttered slightly. "Oh, okay then, cool."

He pulled her into a hug, resting his chin on top of her head and exhaled heavily. "I had a wonderful time, thanks for inviting me." He pulled back and cupped her cheeks. "I'm glad I spent today with you, you're what I'm thankful for."

She smiled at him, her dimples popping.

They went downstairs and he thanked her parents for the invitation and for dinner and said that he needed to leave unexpectedly. He kissed Kayleigh again and then got in his car and headed for home. When he walked in, he let Geralt out for a hop around and hid some of his favorite veggies around the living room before he opened his phone up again.

Matt: Where are youu?
Matt: Why aren't you anwsering me?
Matt: Why sid you leave us?

Followed by fifteen missed calls. It was weird behavior

but what worried Ben the most was the last message from him.

Matt: I get why yuo left now…

Why did this have to happen today? Holidays always felt like a time to be around family, but Ben never felt like he had one he connected with, until today. Kayleigh and her parents had welcomed him with open arms, the warmth from them chasing away the cold upbringing he'd had from his parents. Although Kayleigh and her parents didn't know Ben liked to dress up as a 1950s rock star in his spare time, they still accepted him as he was. So why couldn't he shut his family out? Why did it hurt so much that his brother had contacted him?

Just then his phone buzzed again. With a sigh, he answered.

"Benny?" Matt slurred down the phone.

"Yeah?" he replied, his stomach sinking when he realized just how drunk his brother was. Ben was probably in for an ass-chewing now.

"Where are you?"

"Why do you care?" Ben snapped.

"Because I miss you, lil bro. I miss your face," his brother hiccupped.

"Bullshit," Ben snorted.

"No, it'ss true. I'm sorry about Tammy. I fucked up. I shoulda known she was a user, sshe just seemed so genuine. But you know what they say, these hoes ain't loyal…"

"Don't call her that. Just because she left your sorry ass doesn't give you the right to talk about her like that."

"You gon' def-defend her? After what ssshhhe did to you?"

"People make mistakes. It was you and Dad who made it worse. You humiliated me, forced me to leave because I'm not like you, and made me feel like a failure for not wanting what you both did."

"We don't both want it…" Matt trailed off, his voice small. "It's tough for me too, you know. D'you ever th-think that maybe I didn't want thiss either? That I did it becaussse it was what was expected of me as the older b-brother? The heir? How c-come you get to be the one who does what you want? It'ss not fair!"

"I'm not fighting with you anymore," Ben said, shaking his head though he knew Matt couldn't see him.

"Tha's not why I called. I just…it's Thanksgiving…I miss you."

Ben was about to reply that he missed Matt too, in a weird way, but then the next words came and he couldn't help but feel like Matt was manipulating him.

"Where are you? Tell me where you are?"

"Why, so you can go running to Dad and snitch, like normal?"

"No man, 'cause…'cause I miss you, how many times do I need to tell you?"

Ben sighed, regretting his response before it even came out. "I'm somewhere in Tennessee," he replied.

"Let me guess, Memphis?" The cackle that came down the line made Ben end the call.

How had he and Matt ended up like this? They used to be so close as kids, playing together as a little team. Just the two of them against the world. Well, their parents and the staff. But then as they got older and expectations started piling on them, Matt pulled away, effectively ending their closeness and instead they became like strangers. That was one of the reasons Ben found it so hard to trust people. His own family had shut him out.

He shook his head; he didn't need to think about them anymore. He just wanted Kayleigh, so he went and booted up his computer, ruffling Geralt's long, white mane while he waited to log into the chat.

GoodGirlKay: What did the turkey say to its computer?
GoodGirlKay: Google, Google, Google!
GoodGirlKay: Happy Thanksgiving, bestie xx

Ben's smile stretched wide. Yep, this was exactly what he needed.

Chapter 13

A couple of days later Ben was pacing back and forth in Taylor's office, the volume of the crowd out in the bar twisting his stomach into knots.

It was all Kayleigh's fault he was in this position. If she hadn't been so damn inspiring, he would be at home having boys' night with Geralt. Instead, here he was, examining the profound impact she was having on his life.

Ben had thought himself broken when he arrived in Citrus Pines, eager to seek out his online friend for comfort, to help him lick his wounds and start fresh. But the town and Kayleigh had brought him back to life. Only he was keeping two things from her. The true foundation of their friendship, and his passion for performing. And he couldn't seem to work up the courage to tell her about either.

He would tell her who he really was, and soon. He owed it to her after she had done what he thought was impossible. Watching her grow in confidence and determination had given him the courage to take up performing again, to live his life how he wanted and ignore his family's ridicule. Screw his family's derision. Screw what they thought. Life was feeling good.

Except that he didn't think he could find the words to tell her about it. Not after what happened the last time he revealed his passion to someone. But he could *show* her.

Which was how he found himself, in Taylor's office, dressed in that white satin jumpsuit decorated with gleaming rhinestones, hair slicked back, guitar in hand, and pacing to keep the stage fright at bay.

He had spoken to Taylor, agreed with her that he would be able to perform tonight and see what kind of draw the event was. Last night he opened up his old Twitter and Instagram accounts to post for the first time in months.

@TheKingLivesOn: Live performance at The Rusty Bucket Inn in Citrus Pines, TN. Saturday November 26th at 7pm.

He had messaged Kayleigh, asking her to come to the bar tonight and bring her parents. She wasn't meant to be working, a new girl, Rebelle, was starting her first shift and Taylor was working closely with her. He had also stopped by the diner earlier in the day and asked Ruby to join, he could hear her even now out in the bar, hollering and cackling at various jokes.

His tension mounted, his stage fright grew. Something else he and Elvis shared but when both of them got on stage, they loved it, despite the nerves. Still he needed Kayleigh here like he had never needed anyone before.

There was a knock at the door and his stomach clenched tighter. Taylor poked her head in and Ben remembered how jealous he had been of her when he first arrived. How he'd thought his girl had been in love with her and that he would never stand a chance. Now he could sense Kayleigh felt differently about Taylor, more sisterly than like a lover.

"Holy shit, you look fucking amazing!" Taylor gasped. "I swear, if I wasn't dickmatized by Beau, I would be on you right now."

Ben chuckled. She certainly had a way with words, he'd give her that. *"Thank you very much."*

Taylor's hand flew to her chest. "Be still my beating heart. You had to know what you were doing there, right?"

He chuckled again. The phrase had just slipped out. "Thanks, I think. Is Kayleigh here?"

"Yup, just turned up, parents in tow."

Ben went over to the door and peeked out. Seeing Kayleigh, her little peach head peeking out above the crowd, looking for him, his heart settled, his stomach quieted and he just *knew*. He was ready to bare his soul to her.

"You should probably get out there, Ruby is gonna start a riot soon," Taylor sighed.

He nodded. "I'm ready. Let's do this."

*

Where is he? Kayleigh looked around the packed bar for his blond head but couldn't see him anywhere. She had just finished writing an amazing opening scene to her new story, which may or may not have been inspired by Ben, when she got his message to meet him here and bring her parents.

"Is it always this busy, honey?" her mom asked her.

She shook her head, still looking for Ben. "No, I don't know what's going on."

"I don't even recognize half the people here, they must be from the next county over," her dad replied.

Kayleigh spied Taylor and made a beeline for her, eager to find Ben. She was missing him. It had only been two days since she'd seen him and he'd given her a mind-blowing orgasm that she had yet to reciprocate but two days was a long time when someone was invading your thoughts as much as he was.

"Tay!" she called, but Taylor just pinkie waved at her and proceeded behind the bar, picking up the microphone.

"Good evening, ladies and gentlemen and welcome to a historic evening at The Rusty Bucket Inn! We've had performers here before, but nothing like this, so ladies, hold onto your panties, and men, hold onto your ladies. Please welcome to the stage, the one, the only, Mr. Elvis Presley!"

The whistles and applause were thunderous, shaking the wooden floor of the bar and pandemonium erupted. Kayleigh looked around confused, *What the hell is going on?*

"Elvis, oh boy, we're in for a treat!" her dad yelled over the noise.

"Oh, Kayleigh honey, you didn't tell us Ben was an impersonator!" her mom cried, delight etched across every inch of her face. "My Gosh, he looks fantastic!" she added, and was her mom *squealing*?

"What? What's going on?" Kayleigh muttered to herself, then she saw him. On the stage, lights shining down on his slicked back hair, refracting off the rhinestones that adorned the front of his satin jumpsuit. The split down the middle traveled halfway down his torso and while slim, Ben was toned and spying his chest hair only made him more appealing. He had the kind of build that made her feel safe yet desperate to explore him at the same time. Kayleigh's tongue felt twenty times heavier as she took him in, elbowing her way to the front of the stage to be closer, to get a better look, to just be near him.

How had he never mentioned this? How did she not know?

He plucked the strings of his guitar and the crowd settled down. Then he launched straight into *Hound Dog* and everyone went wild, including Kayleigh. He moved to the music, bouncing on the balls on his feet along with the beat. From *Hound Dog* he went into *Blue Suede Shoes* and then *Jailhouse Rock*. He slowed it down with *Are You Lonesome Tonight?* and *Can't Help Falling In Love*, showcasing a rich, mellow tone, sending shivers down her spine. Clearly, she wasn't the only one affected. All the women were trying not to lose it, except for Ruby who tried to climb onto the stage and had to be tackled by Taylor.

When he sang the last line, his velvet voice echoing out, he looked directly at Kayleigh, and she was captivated. He winked and heat enveloped her, her flush beginning at her neck and traveling down. She suddenly understood why women had gone so crazy over the real deal all those years ago. His eyes locked with hers, like he was trying to communicate something with her. Was he falling in love with her? Her breath stuttered out of her at the prospect, she was certainly falling for him.

He was authentic, unabashedly Elvis, a man who

hadn't even been alive when Ben was born but he encapsulated him perfectly. She had previously only seen slightly pudgy, middle-aged men as Elvis impersonators, not this sexy, young, suave man on stage who was absolutely killing it.

He switched back into up tempo numbers, *Suspicious Minds* and *Burning Love* shimmying and shaking his shoulders, rolling his hips and pelvis in a way that should be downright illegal. The older ladies in the room screamed wildly like they were watching the man himself. Side to side he swung, back and forth until finally he lifted himself up on his tiptoes and rolled his whole body in one smooth wave. Kayleigh tore her eyes from him and looked at the crowd, the ladies either swooning or getting ready to launch themselves at him, and Kayleigh was getting ready to fight them for her man.

He finished his set with *Unchained Melody* to raucous applause and chants for more, more, more. Taylor managed to distract the crowd with alcohol long enough for Kayleigh to fight her way to Ben on stage where she threw herself at him. His arms wrapped around her and squeezed her tight, his body trembling.

She peppered kisses over his face. "You're amazing, that was amazing! I can't…why didn't you tell me?" She tripped over her words in her eagerness to get them out. She stared at him, his eyes wide shimmering pools as he gazed down at her. Something pricked at her. Green eyes. Ben dressed as the King…*green eyes…king*. As quickly as it nudged at her it disappeared.

He pulled her tight against him, still shaking but she heard his words over the noise of the bar.

"I was so scared. So scared you'd laugh at me. That's what Tammy did, when I finally told her. I trusted her with my biggest secret, my passion, and she laughed at me and told my brother. Then he announced it in front of all our family and friends for maximum effect. They humiliated me. I tried to give it up, to stop, to be how they wanted me to be, but I just couldn't. This is in my blood."

She tried to pull back to look at him, to reassure him but he wouldn't let her go. She heard his shuddering breath and held on tight, never wanting to let go of this magnificent man.

After a few moments, his body stopped trembling and he relaxed then slowly his arms loosened from around her and he pulled back. His face was tinged red and his eyes shining, but he quirked his lip up at her, like he was telling her he was okay. She took his hand as they stepped down from the stage

Kayleigh's mother flung herself at him, kissing his cheeks. Ben was very gracious, accepting the mauling, and Kayleigh made a mental note to have a word with her mother about keeping her hands off her man.

"Ben, that was outstanding! I have no words. You were like a carbon copy. Even your voice, so similar!" Maureen patted his cheeks affectionately.

Her father held out his hand and they shook. "Why didn't you mention this the other day, son? I can't believe I sat there like an idiot telling you all about the man when clearly you know a lot about him yourself."

Ben's face fell. "No! Sir, please, that was one of the most thrilling conversations I've had in a while. It meant so much to me, to be able to talk about him with you."

The dip of Ben's brows and his tone drenched with an earnestness you couldn't deny had her father clearing his throat. Albert clapped him on the back and led him over to the bar.

"Now, let's get you a drink, you must be thirsty after

all that hip thrusting," her dad joked, and Kayleigh wanted to die inside, until Ben shot her a look filled with fire.

More patrons came over to congratulate him on his set and ask when the next performance was. It turned out he had a massive following on his socials and there were even some fans who followed him around the country. Kayleigh just watched him, in his element, speaking to his fans, his aura shining vibrantly. Until two men came over to him, both slightly taller and extremely imposing.

"Benjamin? A word. Now." The older man said. Kayleigh took him in, his gray hair perfectly styled, his hard jawline, the stubborn jut of his chin and she would recognize those green eyes anywhere. Ben's father had entered the building.

*

Chapter 14

Ben's stomach sank as he turned to face his father. He looked into his eyes, so similar to Ben's own, only his weren't bathed in disappointment. Hovering behind his father was Matt, a sheepish expression on his face.

"How did you find me?"

His father snorted in derision. "You weren't exactly stealthy. You posted online where you were going to be. It wasn't difficult, Benjamin." Once again, Ben felt about two feet tall under the stern gaze and condescending words. Yes, he had posted online, but he didn't think his father would know how to find his account, let alone have the inclination to actually go out of his way to look for it.

"I guess that's down to you?" Ben spoke to his brother, raising an eyebrow.

"Get changed out of that ridiculous get up, you're coming home." There was no room for argument with the tone, that was how his father had ruled him as a child. The fear of disobeying him and the potential consequences were enough to have Ben do whatever his father told him. But he wasn't a child anymore.

Humiliation crawled across his skin, traveling up his neck to set his cheeks aflame with the knowledge that Kayleigh and her family were witnessing this exchange. Until he felt Kayleigh's hand slip into his and her heat at his side.

"He's not going anywhere," she said, arching an eyebrow at his father, a belligerent expression on her face that he hadn't seen before. Ben had previously thought that she didn't need Kayleigh 2.0, she just needed to believe in herself and not accept the way people treated her. Which is exactly what she was doing and he was damn grateful in that moment that she had his back. His father's bored gaze flicked to Kayleigh, running over her before dismissing her, and that set Ben's blood aflame.

"Time to end this little temper tantrum, Benjamin. The clinic needs you. You never think things through. You dropped out of med school on a whim, quit your training as a paramedic and moved to some random backwater town without speaking to anyone about it, just because your feelings got hurt? What's the matter with you? We're Morgans and this is not how we handle our shit!" His father bellowed, so loud that Ben flinched and so did Matt who was looking suitably apologetic, hiding away behind their father.

A number of people opened their mouths to reply but one was louder than the rest.

"I don't know where you're from, pal, but that isn't the way we speak to our children in our *backwater town*.

Now I suggest, unless you're looking for some kind of trouble, that you turn around and march your fancy ass right outta here."

Ben was shocked to see it was Kayleigh's father by his side, folding his arms over his barrel chest. Ben looked around, seeing Maureen and Albert side by side, ready to protect him, along with Kayleigh and Taylor. Even Ruby was cracking her knuckles. Love filled him at the way this town was willing to fight his battle, to support him. He had done nothing but love and support his family and they took the one thing he loved and used it to humiliate him, he didn't owe them anything.

Pulling confidence from Kayleigh and those around him, he faced his father down.

"Yeah, march your fancy ass outta here, Pops. I'm already home."

"Dammit Benjamin, there's that smart mouth of yours. You're making a big mistake staying here."

"That smart mouth of his is my favorite thing about him and he clearly didn't get it from you, now get outta my bar and take your sad sidekick with you," Taylor nodded towards Matt who had the gall to look affronted.

"Yeah, get out of our bar," Kayleigh added, and Ben squeezed her hand tight. Seeing the locals rallying around his son, his father shook his head before spinning on his designer booted heel and leaving, with Matt towing along behind him.

Ben tried to feel an ounce of guilt or remorse, but his father hadn't come here to apologize and give his blessing or have some big family reunion. He had come here to *rescue* Ben, to bring him home, like he'd been having a break and was ready to rejoin the legacy his father had built. The only guilt that pricked at Ben was seeing Matt kowtow, but Matt had made his bed. Ben knew he was the only reason his father had found him, he never would have looked at social media on his own.

With the drama over, Maureen, clearly loving the display that Albert put on, tugged him over to a dark corner of the bar and Kayleigh spun away immediately. "Ew."

Ben laughed and pulled her into a hug and brushed his lips softly over hers. "Thank you, a thousand times, thank you."

She sank into his embrace and ran her tongue over his lips, the wet sensation sending his pulse skyrocketing. She broke the kiss, far sooner than he had intended and he dove right back down to continue but her hand against his mouth stopped him.

"Come with me," she murmured and took his arm, pulling him towards the back door of the bar once again. He followed her blindly, desperate to be alone with her. He felt raw, cut open and vulnerability was pouring out but he only wanted her. As soon as the cool air hit them, he was pressing her against the wall, attacking her mouth with his, his hot wet tongue invading until she was squirming against him, pulling at his jumpsuit with desperate hands.

"Fuck me, please?" she moaned, and damn if he didn't die and go to heaven right there.

"Say please again," he growled.

Her eyes dragged to his, glittering like the depths of the ocean. "Please," she breathed, and his eyes fluttered closed, his cock pulsing beneath the satin, desperate to finally be inside her. He pulled back, tugging at his costume, annoyed at the lack of flexibility.

She giggled as he struggled. "Do you think Elvis had this problem?"

"Kay, there are times when I'm really happy to talk

about Elvis, but this isn't one of them. Sonofa-" he shouted, finally getting himself free. He tugged it down, so it pooled around his waist and she reached out, stroking her fingers over his chest, tugging at the short hair there. He knew he wasn't as buff as some guys but the way she looked at him made him feel like a God.

"Wrap your legs around my waist," he said, lifting her up, light as a feather. He found her mouth again, nipping and licking at her until something occurred to him. He pulled away and she huffed in annoyance.

He looked around them. "What if we get caught again?"

She pressed herself against him and rolled her hips. "Isn't that part of the excitement?" she husked, nipping at his lip.

"Kayleigh Good being so bad," he murmured, feeding her another kiss. Then pulling away again, in frustration, his hand slapping the side of the building. "I don't have anything."

"Oh, I do!" It was only then that he noticed she still had her purse draped across her body and he had never been more grateful. She rummaged in it, producing a foil packet like she had just struck gold after months of searching. He took it from her with one hand, the other still wrapped around her as he leaned her more firmly against the wall to prop her up. He tore the packet open with his teeth and pushed his jumpsuit down to his knees, and after some deft movements managed to roll the condom on.

He flipped up the bottom of her white dress then gripped her chin, tilting her mouth up to meet his, sliding his tongue in and out of her slowly as he worked himself inside. Her soft, breathy exhalations tickled him and nearly broke all his restraint. When he was seated inside her, he kissed her fully until she became impatient and tried to thrust. He hissed and then pulled back and thrust into her deeply, earning him a startled cry which turned into a moan part way through. He worked his hips, in and out, slowly until she gripped the back of his neck tight, her fingers twisting in his hair.

"I said, fuck me, Ben," she commanded, her voice low, her eyes glazed with passion.

"Yes, ma'am," he grunted and then proceeded to do just that. He pounded into her, bouncing her up and down. "Pull your dress down, I want to see you," he growled. She did exactly as told, and when her breast was free he sucked a nipple into his mouth, his hand delving beneath her skirt to the place they were joined and traced slick circles around her clit.

She cried out and he hoped like hell no one heard her and came looking for them. He continued his torment on her body and it wasn't long before she was crying out and shuddering around him. He thrust into her tight flesh again and again, his release creeping up on him, snapping at the base of his spine until he buried his face in her neck and bit down as he grunted, filling the condom.

Their panting breaths filled the space around them, and in that moment he had never known such bliss, Kayleigh wrapped around him, their hearts racing together.

"I love you."

It slipped out, entirely without his permission. She stiffened and pulled away, brushing his hair back and lifting his chin so she could look into his eyes. He knew what she would see: his unadulterated love, stripped bare. It would be startling, the force of it. Terrifying if she wasn't ready for it, he just hoped to hell she was.

"I'm sorry, I didn't mean to scare you. It's okay if you

don't feel it too. And I know after sex is the *worst* time to say that. But it's true, please don't believe it isn't. I've loved you for a while now," he added, his rawness not stopping his tongue from running away with itself.

She cupped his jaw and placed a delicate kiss at the corner of his mouth. "I'm not scared and although I'm not there yet, I'm on my way. I'll let you know when I am there, I promise you that."

Even though it wasn't a declaration of love, it was close and he would take it, would snatch it with greedy hands and fingers and hold onto it tight.

"Come home with me?" he breathed against the shell of her ear. She shuddered and her whispered *yes* reached his love fogged brain and moments later, they were in his car on the way home.

*

Chapter 15

Had a man dressed as Elvis just rocked her entire world? Yes. Emphatically yes.

He loved her.

She could feel it in the way he touched her, see it in the way he looked at her and she was falling too. She hadn't quite reached the love destination, but it was on the horizon and only getting closer.

The journey back to his house felt too long as she kept shooting him sideways looks and each time, he just squeezed her hand like he was responding to questions she hadn't asked.

Yes, this is happening.
Yes, everything is fine.
Yes, I do really love you.

But one question on her mind had her breaking the

silence. "Why Elvis?"

Ben shrugged in that familiar way and squeezed her hand again. "He bucked trends and was always told he would never amount to anything. He didn't do what people expected of him and after all the stuff with my family, I kinda relate. That and the music. Young Elvis did these incredible, catchy pop songs that transcended boundaries. Older Elvis did the same thing but also these soulful broken songs. He was a man of growth, just like I want to be."

"I love that," she replied, smiling over at him.

The reminder of his family had her wondering how he felt about the scene with his dad and brother. She'd seen the vulnerability on his face when they appeared and she had wanted protect him from their unfeeling, mean words.

Then they had gone outside and taken their relationship to the next level. He had been amazing, she had never had an orgasm that intense with any of her previous partners, both men and women. Her body was still humming for him even now and she didn't think she would ever get enough of this man.

As soon as he pulled up outside the one-story brick house, he ran around to her door and opened it, tugging her out and into his arms with an urgency she matched. They fell through the front door, kissing, barely coming up for air but long enough for her to mutter *bedroom* and he took her straight there. She would look around the place in the morning, right now, she just needed him.

They collapsed onto the bed and giggled together before furiously attacking each other's mouths again. He stripped off her cardigan, his hands delving under her dress and into her panties which were already wet with her desire for him. He pulled her on top of him, thrusting up into her and she struggled to get the tight satin suit down his arms.

She laughed, pulling away. "I can't do it, I'm too weak. Take it off."

He tugged it down his arms, gripping her hips and lifting her so he could pull it all the way off and then he was gloriously naked.

"You don't wear underwear underneath?" she asked, curious.

"Sometimes but not with this one, don't want those visible panty lines," he shrugged, and she burst out laughing, holding her stomach as it ached with mirth.

"It's really not nice to laugh at a naked man," he grumbled. She stopped and kissed him before scooting back to sit on his thighs, looking down at his naked body. Her laughter died in her throat as she took in his cock, hard and reaching up towards his stomach.

"It's very lovely," she breathed. *Ugh, had she really said, lovely?*

"Thank you," he chuckled, reaching for her but she pressed down on his chest firmly. He had been in her bedroom and pleasured her with his mouth and now she was going to do the same. She scooted back further and dipped her head, her breath teasing over the soft skin. She looked up at him from under her lashes and his expression was fixed, his shoulders tense, ready for her mouth. One lick had his hands delving into her hair, his head tipping back and a ragged groan left his lips. All thoughts fled her brain except one: *make him yours.*

She worked her mouth over him, from base to tip, using her tongue, her hands and feeling wanton at his reaction to what she was doing. Seeing how much he enjoyed it had pride bubbling inside her. The tendrils of confidence that had sprouted from her pole dancing classes continued unfurling in the wake of her ability to make him feel this good. This was her. Not Kayleigh 2.0 but Regular Kayleigh. Seeing him writhing in pleasure as she licked and squeezed, her name tumbling from his lips like falling stars. She had done this to him, only her. Driven him to this wild ecstasy with her mouth.

"God, Kayleigh," he grunted, thrusting gently into her mouth. She moaned in response, and he stilled, his hand tensed in her hair as he panted. He cupped her jaw, drawing her gaze up to meet his and when their eyes locked, he shuddered, and she tasted him on her tongue. He pulled her into his arms, and they lay wrapped in each other. Just before she succumbed to sleep, she heard his whispered, *I love you.*

*

Kayleigh woke up early in the morning, her eyes taking in the unfamiliar surroundings before she remembered where she was, who she was with and the activities from the previous evening. A satisfied smile found its way onto her lips and she rolled over, seeing Ben laying on his side, facing away from her. She scooted over, pressing a kiss to his shoulder, his skin warm and inviting. His breathing deepened but he gave no other reaction.

Movement at the foot of the bed had her frowning, she peered down and came face to face with a white, long-haired rabbit with floppy ears.

She giggled. "Hello you."

The rabbit gave no reaction save a little nose twitch. Then leaped into the air, twisted its body and landed in the same spot. *What was that?* She reached out her hand and the rabbit hopped forward and sniffed her, before its little tongue darted out and licked her. The rasp of its tongue tickled her, then the rabbit jumped off the bed and disappeared. How come Ben never mentioned he had a rabbit?

She lay there for a little while, daydreaming until her bladder began complaining so she got up and left the room searching for the bathroom. The house was small but cozy, with thick navy carpet throughout and pale gray walls. It was still dark, so she felt along the walls for a light switch. She found a door handle and opened it, fumbling along the wall for the light, hoping she had found the bathroom.

When the room lit up she could see she hadn't, it was his study. She was about to leave but spotted an oak sideboard with a record player and stack of old records that must have been from his grandma. Then she spotted his computer. He had been eager to see hers and she realized she was just as eager to see his. To see if he had the same set up as her or any components she was missing. Looking at the computer reminded her she hadn't logged on last night and spoken to her friend. That was the first time they had missed each other since her break after the accident at work.

She was distracted from thinking about him when she saw Ben's mouse. It was black with metallic silver down the sides and dome shaped like the hood of a sleek sportscar, it was fancy as hell. She lifted it, to inspect it, definitely not jealous of it at all. The movement of the mouse lit up the screen and filled the room. Kayleigh shielded her stare from the bright light and then she saw the screen. There was a document open, and she averted her eyes, not wanting to read his private things but she had already recognized it. Her eyes swung back to it.

Her Romeo and Juliet story.

"What the hell?" she murmured in the quiet room.

How the hell had he got a copy of this? That niggling sensation prickled her again as she scrolled through the document and noticed comments. The name next to the comment had her gasping.

GreenEyedKing96.

"No," she breathed, covering her mouth with her hand. "No, no way." Her body went numb with shock, but she couldn't accept it. She minimized the document and looked for the icon she knew would reveal everything. When she spotted it, she opened up the chat where it already had his username pre-filled, it just needed his password.

"No!" she cried, pushing herself away and in the process, she tripped and fell back. How could it be *him*? She didn't understand. Surely, he wouldn't lie to her? Wouldn't hide his identity from her? He had said he loved her. Someone who loved you wouldn't keep such a huge secret. She sat there, shaking her head until she felt something tickle her foot. She looked down and spotted the white rabbit, licking her ankle and thought of GreenEyedKing96's avatar, a white rabbit.

Her heart sank.

*

Ben woke up slowly, reluctant to be pulled from his dreams of Kayleigh in his arms, in his bed. Except she *was* in his bed. She was finally his. And he was performing again. Relief flooded him, everything was perfect. *Nearly perfect*, his subconscious piped up, reminding him he still needed to talk to her about their history. He knew he needed to tell her but not today. Today he would love her until she couldn't breathe any longer without thinking about him.

Love Me Good

He stretched the long luxurious stretch of a man full of happiness. Then he sat up in bed, rubbing his eyes and as his vision cleared, he saw her, his bad girl, sitting in the armchair in the corner of the room, petting Geralt who rested in her lap. Her peach hair perfectly kinked around her shoulders, her lush mouth plump from being nibbled but her eyes… her eyes were hard.

He paused. "Kayleigh?"

"Who's Kayleigh?" Her facial expression didn't change, her mouth barely moved but there was a chill in her words that he felt to his bones.

His brows tugged down in confusion. "What do you mean?"

"Don't you mean, GoodGirlKay?"

Although he hadn't eaten anything yet, his stomach roiled, ready to empty itself and he stopped cold. Silence stretched between them as he worked out how the hell to handle this. She waited patiently. He could sense her guard was up, she was coiled, ready to strike at him and he needed to handle this carefully.

He held out his hands, pleadingly. "Kay, I know how it looks. I was going to tell you, I swear it. But I didn't know how to come out and say 'Hey, I'm your friend online who *didn't* move halfway across the country to be near you'."

Her eyebrows flew up. "Are you seriously trying to be funny right now?"

He scrubbed a hand over his face. "No, honestly no. I'm scared and don't know how to handle this. I love you, Kay. Please."

She scoffed and shot up from the chair, grabbing her shoes that she had kicked off last night in their desperation to get to bed. God, he'd give anything to go back to then and fix this before it got out of hand.

"So you've just been pretending to be someone else?"

"No! That's not it at all, I don't need to pretend to be someone else."

She reared back, her mouth dropping open. "What, like me you mean?"

"No, Kayleigh, that's not what I meant at all. I just meant I didn't change how I acted from the guy you knew online because that *is* me and I wanted you to connect with the real me."

"This isn't something you do to someone you love. How could you keep this from me? Did you think I wouldn't find out? That I wouldn't notice? Oh my God, that's why you pulled back online, isn't it? I feel sick." She paused, pressing a hand to her mouth.

His heart ached. He made her feel sick? That was not good, at all. Desperation began nipping at his heels.

"Yes, but only because I didn't want to continue developing a relationship online, I wanted to do it in person, for real. I couldn't mess you around and play with your feelings. You're my best friend in the whole world, you mean so much more to me than words could ever express. I came here for you. I needed to escape my family and reset my life, and the way you talked about this place, the pull it had, and you being here…I just needed to see, see what could happen." He was rambling but his words only made her put her shoes on faster and his panic began to spiral.

"Kay, please. So many times, you said you wished I could move here, so I did."

She stood up and pointed a finger at him. "You *used* me! You faked it. *Everything*. God, I'm such an idiot that I didn't even put two and two together and realize I was talking to the same person. It makes so much sense now, the connection I felt for you, how it felt like I had known you so long, how *right* you felt. Christ, I'm an idiot!"

"No, you're not. You're perfect and kind and luminous and *everything*. Kayleigh, you're everything."

He tried to take her hand, but she pulled it out of his grasp. "Don't touch me right now."

"Please, you have to know. This was only ever meant to be about caring for you. That all I wanted was a chance."

"You really don't see what you did?" A tear slipped down her cheek, gutting him.

"I do, I do see it. I was going to tell you, I swear."

"When? When we fucked a third time?" He flinched at her words. "When we got married? When we had *kids*?"

She headed for the door and he was close behind her, his desperation pushing him forward. "Please don't leave, let's talk about this?"

"I have nothing to say to you. You said I was your friend. You pushed me and supported me and I was falling for you. I defended you against your family, and this whole time you were keeping it secret that we already knew each other? That I had known you for *two years*? I can't even be around you right now."

With that she left the room and he stood there, reeling from her words. In the distance the front door slammed, and he sank onto the bed wondering how his life had gone from glorious to empty in five minutes flat.

*

Chapter 16

Kayleigh swiped furiously at her tears, trying to stop the little whimpers from slipping out as she walked past people from town who tried to ask if she was okay. She didn't want to speak to anyone because she wasn't okay. She had just discovered that someone who had burrowed under her skin, that she'd let inside her, had been keeping something huge from her.

She had got over the Elvis thing. The fact that he didn't tell her about his passion that was such a huge part of his life had hurt, but she understood why, when he had shared what happened the last time he told someone. He didn't owe her an explanation about that. But this?

She felt like she had been betrayed two times over. Firstly by the physical, standing right in front of her, kissing her and loving her Ben. Secondly by the non-

Love Me Good

physical, words on a screen, backbone of her life GreenEyedKing96. Except they were the same person.

She couldn't wrap her head around it but at the same time it made perfect sense. The feeling she got when talking to them both, the warmth from them, the care. The interest in her life and pushing her to get herself out there and have confidence in her writing.

No wonder GreenEyedKing96 hadn't wanted to video call with her: then the jig would be up. Fresh pain stroked over her already sore wounds and her hurt crept ever higher. He knew, yet he continued the ruse even after. Her cheeks flushed as she remembered when their online relationship had taken a turn, where he'd gotten sexual and then immediately pulled back. She scoffed, *well at least that makes sense now.*

She made it home and taking a shuddering breath she went inside the house.

"Morning sweetheart," her mom called. Kayleigh could hear her pattering around the living room and hurried past the open doorway, heading towards the stairs.

"I'm not feeling well so I'm gonna go to bed for a little while," she called and rushed up the stairs to her room before her mom could reply. She shut the door and leaned back against it, releasing her breath, her eyes darting around the room, lingering on her computer and then her bed, where she had memories of Ben. She clapped her hands over her eyes and scrubbed, desperate to shake the images free.

She turned her computer on, the messenger app automatically loading and logging her in. It was a reflex. When she was down, she needed GreenEyedKing96 to talk to, to get all her woes out and for him to build her back up again. She needed her friend. She realized what she had done and was about to shut the system back down when the message alerts popped up.

GreenEyedKing96: Kayleigh, please, let me explain!
GreenEyedKing96: You have EVERY right to be mad and I'm so, so sorry, trust me when I say I know exactly what I did and why it's so awful. I don't know how to fix it. I don't know how to make it right but please trust that I'm sorry.
GreenEyedKing96: I never wanted to hurt you, you're everything to me, everything.
GreenEyedKing96: Please don't shut me out, let's talk.
GreenEyedKing96: I love you xx

She hovered her mouse over his screen name, over his bunny avatar and right-clicked. The drop-down menu came up and she hovered over the word for a moment, second guessing herself before finally clicking *block*.

Then she truly cried, great heaving sobs that racked her small chest. She crawled into bed, hugging her pillow tightly and when her tears finally subsided, she was numb to the pain. She continued to lay there until sleep crept in, soothing her for a few hours, giving her heart and emotions the break they needed.

When she awoke hours later, she got ready for work, showering and dressing with empty, stilted movements. She said goodbye to her parents and set off on her bicycle for the bar. It was only as the bar came into view that she considered she would see him. Ben wasn't due to work today but what if he came in anyway, knowing she would be there? Her heart pounded, feelings prodding at her, excitement that she would see him immediately overpowered by hurt at what he'd done and how he'd ruined things for them.

She secured her bike and went inside, the sounds and smells of the place where she spent most of her time wrapped around her in a comforting cloak. Taylor appeared, dressed in a royal blue knit dress, her red curls secured into a loose knot at the top of her head and Kayleigh was struck again by how beautiful she was. But now it felt different, more like Kayleigh could appreciate her beauty without unrequited feelings overwhelming her; they were gone. She wished she could say the same for her feelings for Ben.

Taylor looked up when Kayleigh came closer. "Hey, girl!" Then her happy expression fell, her brows knitted together and her mouth pulled into a tight line. "What's wrong?"

Kayleigh feared this would happen, she knew she would be fine as long as no one asked her what was wrong but the second that happened, all bets were off. Her face crumpled.

"We'll just be two secs," Taylor said to the slim, petite brunette who Kayleigh hadn't even noticed until now. She remembered Taylor saying she had hired Rebelle, another woman from town. *Great, you just make all the best impressions when you meet the new hires, don't you?* Her first encounter with Ben pushing front and center of her mind, and a small sob slipped out. It had been a disastrous meeting, she wasn't even conscious for half of it, but she remembered how he had cared for her, how gentle he had been and his soft expression when he looked at her.

Taylor's arm slipped around Kayleigh's shoulders and steered her into the office and closed the door.

"What did he do? Am I gonna have to fire him?"

"No!" Kayleigh cried, knowing how much this job

meant to Ben.

"What happened?" Taylor offered her a tissue.

"We just had a fight, that's all. We're not together anymore. He didn't hurt me physically if that's what you're worried about."

Taylor's posture lost some of its rigidity and Kayleigh felt bad that she was so worried. "Honestly, just a standard breakup, you know how hard those can be. I just need some time."

"Do you want me to rework your shifts so you're not on together? Well, maybe once in a while you will be, but a majority I could try and fix?"

Kayleigh gave her a small smile, grateful that she would be willing to do that, but she could never put her personal drama ahead of Taylor's business. "No, honestly you don't need to do that, I don't want it affecting work or your business."

Taylor pulled her into a hug. "Sweet Kayleigh Good still always putting everyone else first. I wouldn't have offered if I couldn't do it. We have Rebelle helping out now so that will ease things."

Kayleigh pulled back to look up at Taylor, she was a tall woman anyway compared to Kayleigh's non-impressive five feet but with the added height of her boots, she towered over Kayleigh, overwhelming her. "You sure?"

"Of course. You're family, and family always comes first."

"I'm not the only one here who puts other people first," Kayleigh grumbled.

Taylor pushed her away playfully. "True, but don't tell anyone. I've spent years cultivating a certain impression of myself and I ain't blowing it now." She winked at Kayleigh and pivoted her towards the door. "Now, git.

I've got some schedules to rework."

"Thanks, Tay," Kayleigh replied as she headed out to introduce herself properly to Rebelle.

*

The days seemed to drag, especially now she wasn't coming home each night and speaking to Ben online. So many times her mouse had hovered over that *unblock* button but she couldn't do it.

She missed him, *hard*. Like a chunk of her soul was gone but she continued to exist, acting like she didn't have a piece of her missing and no idea how to plug that empty space inside. The only good thing to come out of this was that to exorcize her pain, she had been writing: the best thing yet, in her opinion. She had been so excited and desperate to share it with someone and the first person that came to mind, she wasn't speaking to.

She hadn't seen him, and if she was truly honest with herself, she was disappointed that he had stayed away. She was expecting to have him turn up here at the bar or at her house or message her phone but nothing. She knew she was being ridiculous, he had hurt her after all, and she had told him to leave her alone, and sent a very clear message when she blocked him. So why did she still want to see him so bad?

"There's someone here to see you," Rebelle called softly, her words halting and nervous like they were every time she spoke. She was intriguing. Rebelle didn't share any personal information about herself despite Kayleigh asking, but she seemed sweet enough.

Kayleigh stood up from where she had been stacking liquor bottles in the storeroom. Her heart began its excited pound at the prospect of Ben finally coming to her. She tried to tell herself that she wasn't happy at the idea that he had come to her, that she was still mad, still hurt and feeling betrayed but she *missed* him. She smoothed her hands over the front of her dress and came out to the main bar area but he wasn't there, instead she saw Christy.

"We need to talk." The petite blond now had an unreadable expression. Her hands were planted firmly on rounded hips and in one of her hands, Kayleigh saw a manuscript, *her* manuscript. She gulped and nodded, nausea churning in her stomach. Christy marched off into Taylor's office, leaving Kayleigh to trail behind her.

Christy closed the door behind them, Taylor looking up from her desk confused.

"Taylor, get out," Christy commanded.

Taylor sputtered. "It's my office!"

Christy huffed. "Okay fine, stay then, but you're about to get mad in a sec." Christy waved a nonchalant hand and Kayleigh fought a smile as she watched the dynamic unfold between these two best friends. Taylor sat back, folding her arms across her chest, raising a curious eyebrow.

Christy turned to her. "Kayleigh, quit your job. Right this second."

"Hey!" Taylor cried, sitting up.

"I warned you!" Christy jabbed a finger at Taylor who was now pouting. "Kay, this is one of the most amazing things I have ever read. I need to play the game, right this very second and I have *never* gamed in my whole life. So, what the hell are you waiting for, girl?" Christy demanded, raising Kayleigh's manuscript in the air.

"I..." She had no reply.

Christy was determined to hold her to account. She began inspecting her immaculate nails and tapping her foot. "I'm waiting…"

The dam that held all her creative fears inside Kayleigh broke. "I don't know how to do it. I don't know if I *can* do it. I don't know if my story ideas would run dry, and I'm scared. I'm just a normal girl with big unrealistic dreams and this is crazy, to think that I could do this! There, are you happy now?"

"Yes, very. First things first, you're going to go home and research how to do it and what you would need. If you can't get those things or they aren't possible then we will look at how to do this on your own, independently, which I can help you with. The main thing is you stop telling yourself you can't, and start working out all the ways you *can*."

"I would listen to her if I was you Kayleigh, she knows what she's talking about," Taylor piped up.

Kayleigh rolled her eyes. "Now you agree with her? She just told me to quit!"

Taylor frowned. "Oh, yeah."

There was more arguing between the two of them and Kayleigh managed to slip back out to the bar where she could gather her thoughts. Taylor emerged from her office a while later when Rebelle took her break. Taylor was drying glasses and stacking them, but her eyes were on Kayleigh, watching her, following her until finally Kayleigh snapped.

"Okay, say whatever it is you want to say! Are you mad about what happened earlier?"

Taylor put her towel down and faced Kayleigh. "Ben told me what he did."

Kayleigh's throat closed. "Wh- He did?"

"Yup."

"And?"

"He did a shitty thing, that's for sure. You have every

right to be mad at him. I would be. But we've gotten to know Ben, he's a kind and gentle soul. He felt such a connection to you and this town that he changed his whole life."

"But-"

"I ain't finished. Now, I get you're mad and that's fine, he should have been honest with you, about everything, including the Elvis thing. So if you don't think you can move on from this, that's okay. But if you're just being stubborn and letting your pride hold you back from true happiness then you're only getting in your own way. Seeing you two together was something special and I don't want you to throw it away like I nearly did."

Having just witnessed Taylor go through her own personal relationship drama, Kayleigh understood exactly what she meant.

"*You're* something special, Kay and just for the record, I also believe you could do the writing thing. I just didn't say it earlier because I was mad at Christy for telling you to quit. But if that's the right thing for you, I support you, one hundred and ten percent."

"I used to be in love with you," Kayleigh blurted out in response to Taylor's kind words.

Taylor's eyebrows winged up. Then her gaze softened. "I'm not surprised, I'm really awesome."

Kayleigh barked out a laugh and Taylor pulled her into a hug.

That night Kayleigh sat in her room, mulling over Christy's words. Christy believed in her, Taylor believed in her, and so did Ben. So, was she being ridiculous? Were her doubts making her stand in her own way? Was she stopping herself from being the person she wanted to be?

Yes, she thought. A resounding *yes*.

Love Me Good

Kayleigh 2.0 wouldn't put up with these doubts and this bullshit, she would be living and writing and getting herself out there. Suddenly the thought of Kayleigh 2.0 didn't feel right. Who even was Kayleigh 2.0? Some version of herself she created so that she could feel safer in owning her confidence and taking what she wanted? Why should she have to create an alter ego to do that? She shouldn't be afraid to be confident, to go after what she wanted and take up space. Neither of the two main influences in her life, Taylor and Ben, would be afraid.

Ben had done so much for her in the two months they'd been hanging out. He'd pushed her outside of her comfort zone and shown her what she could achieve if she just set her mind to it. She had grown in confidence and started to believe in herself. And watching him as he had owned his passion, his Elvis-ness, taking control of what he wanted had inspired her to do the same. He had given her confidence and helped her to grow as a person.

Ben had loved her long before he even knew Kayleigh 2.0 existed. She didn't need Kayleigh 2.0, Kayleigh 2.0 wasn't separate to her, she *was* her. The best version of herself.

With that realization, Kayleigh logged onto her computer and started researching what she needed to do to start living the life she deserved. Then once she had figured out her path, she started typing up a letter she didn't want to write but needed to, nonetheless.

*

Chapter 17

She'd blocked him.

The action spoke volumes.

Ben waited until she got home, didn't chase after her like his pounding blood told him to, that would do no good, she was too upset, too angry with him to listen and rightfully so. He would wait and see if she came online and try to speak to her then. Thirty minutes later when she did, he immediately messaged her, having zero patience, zero chill. Because when you could feel the love of your life slipping between your fingers, patience didn't exist.

All those messages were read, then a few moments later they were gone. The whole chat was gone. GoodGirlKay was gone. He blinked, hoping it was a trick of his eyes.

"What the f-" he muttered, tapping frantically at his mouse. Closing and opening chats, typing her name in the search bar, nothing. He typed different iterations of her screen name and each time, nothing.

His heart pounded in his chest; his stomach clenched up tight, ready to accept the blow.

She had blocked him. She wanted nothing to do with him. He had hurt her so much she wanted to erase him and the last two years from her life. He sat in his chair, staring at the blank screen that claimed to not know who GoodGirlKay was until the sun began to set and Geralt was tugging at his pants leg.

He bent down, ruffling the bunny's fluff then lifted Geralt into his arms, hugging him tight. The long fur tickled his nose and eyes, but he didn't care. He needed comfort and to work out how the hell to fix what he'd broken.

His body demanded he leap into action, that he go around and see her. That he message her or call her, that he turn up at the bar during her shift to see her. But that block…that told him she didn't want that. His body fought against his instinct to act while his mind calmed itself and accepted that she needed space. After what he'd done the least he could do was respect her wishes.

So he did, he waited that night, then the second night, the hours ticking by painfully slowly. So slowly he was suddenly grateful for the bottle of Tennessee whiskey he'd bought to celebrate moving in. The whole bottle was gone that night while he played various miserable songs. He was such a cliché.

The next day he paid for every mouthful. He spent the morning vomiting while Geralt sat in the corner of the bathroom, his little nose twitching with disappointment. Then Ben showered and napped, and by the time he was getting ready for his shift, he felt almost normal. If you ignored the aching chasm in his chest which whiskey had not filled at all.

The only bright light on the horizon was that if he got to the bar early enough, he might see Kayleigh as they crossed over on their shifts. He was excited to see her but there was a tremor of fear. If she rejected him at all, he would crumble, right there in front of her. He had faced so much rejection from his ex, Tammy, and his family, that if Kayleigh pushed him away, he didn't know if he would recover.

He entered the bar, the noise engulfing him and jolting him out of his mind. He had been alone with his own thoughts, in silence, apart from heart-breaking ballads blaring through his house last night, and he wasn't used to noise. It was surprisingly comforting, but as he looked around the packed bar, down the hallway to the kitchen and back toward Taylor's office, his comfort disappeared. *She's already gone.*

"I've changed some shifts around." Ben turned as Taylor appeared in the doorway of her office. "Figured that maybe it wasn't the best thing for you and Kayleigh to be working together."

He swallowed thickly, her unreadable expression making his mouth drier than the Sahara. "She told you?"

"She just said that you'd broken up and I offered to make things a little easier for both of you."

He nodded. "So, I get to keep my job?"

"As far as I'm concerned, based on the brief explanation she gave, it's just a standard breakup which is awkward as ass and horrible for you both, but I have no qualms about you being here still. Unless you want to elaborate on anything?"

Ben hadn't really made any friends here, except for

Kayleigh. He knew some of the people in the town but didn't consider himself close to any of them yet. Ruby maybe, but all she tried to do when she saw him was figure out how she knew him. Apparently when he'd donned his Elvis costume and performed, it all clicked into place for her. Not surprisingly, she and Elvis had a thing at one time.

But Taylor was different, she had been welcoming and open. She had gotten to know him and if there was one person who would set him straight, it was her. So, he told her everything. Purged his confession and his guilt, his secrets to her and she listened, she didn't comment or interrupt or send him away and at the end she just sighed.

"Well, you definitely fucked up, there's no denying that. She's hurting right now but give her time, she'll cool off and then you can try again to explain it to her. In the meantime, though, I will respect both of your feelings and keep your shifts apart to give you both some time."

"I appreciate that, and you listening. I don't really know anyone here and I know how much Kayleigh means to you," he said.

"She means the world, she's family. But, I guess, so are you."

He lifted his head, a small smile teasing his lips. "Yeah?"

He remembered how she defended him against his father only a few nights ago, how she had supported him and had his back. Sometimes family wasn't someone who shared your blood and DNA.

She sat back down at her desk and began sifting through paperwork, not meeting his gaze. "Yeah. Just don't fuck up again, and don't get all mushy about it either. Now get back to work."

He mock-saluted her. "Yes, ma'am."

*

Ben dreamt of Kayleigh constantly, replaying their last moments. The look on her face as she watched him perform. The way she defended him against his father, held his hand and stood by him. The way she so easily gave him the things he needed, acceptance and support. The way she wrapped herself around him and breathed his name as she shattered in his arms. And why was Kayleigh on her knees, saying his dick was 'lovely' the hottest thing he had ever seen?

He needed her, like air to breathe. He ached for her, an ache that wasn't going anywhere, he was going to have to learn to live with it. Over a week had passed and he was still too scared to reach out to her, too scared to talk to her in case she rejected him again. He passed his time at work, his shifts fleeting, with lots of customers all commenting on his performance and eager to know when the next one was but he had no clue. Right now, he wasn't exactly feeling inspired.

His socials had blown up when he announced his return performance. There was definitely an appetite for more and normally that would have given him a thrill, that unparalleled high but right now, joy was muted because he was missing her. Each time the door to the bar opened, a beat of hope thudded his heart and then stalled when it wasn't her who stepped through it.

Taylor kept assuring him that she would come around, but he had lost hope.

Then one afternoon, he was placing an invoice on Taylor's desk when he saw it. Kayleigh's resignation letter, all typed up nice and neat. Even though a font wasn't personal, seeing her words sent reminders flooding

Love Me Good

through him of all their messages. Because she had blocked him, he couldn't even look through their old chats, and he berated himself for never saving them.

He stormed back out to the bar, the notice in his hand and confronted Taylor. "Were you gonna tell me about this?"

She arched a perfect brow at him "Excuse you? Last I checked, you weren't the owner."

He drew back, telling himself to calm down. "She can't leave, she just can't!"

"Ben-" Taylor began but he cut her off.

"No!" His fear grew, panic clutching at his chest. "She can't leave us, she can't leave *me*."

He needed to see her now. He dropped the letter and ran out of the bar, getting into his car and driving over to her house. He pulled up outside, glancing up at the building. In his panic, he hadn't worked out what he was going to say. How could he face her? How could he demand she stay here when he knew she had dreams she wanted to achieve? Dreams that didn't involve working at the bar.

Ben saw the curtain twitch in the window and two seconds later the front door opened, and her father stepped out. Albert walked down the path and stopped in front of Ben's window which he reluctantly lowered, ready to face whatever her father was going to say.

"She's not here," Albert said, his voice gruff.

"Oh, okay then." Ben said, lamely.

"She's not been happy lately, is that to do with you?"

"Yes."

Albert harumphed. "Well, what are you gonna do to fix it?"

Ben had been poised, ready for a verbal attack and prepared to accept it. Instead, her father was offering hope.

Ben lifted his eyes to meet Albert's. "You think I have a chance?"

"Well, I can't say for sure, only she can say that. So, you'd best get to talking. We liked having you around. You were real good for each other." And with that he turned around and went back into the house, leaving Ben to contemplate what the hell to do. He needed to be more like Kayleigh and have the guts to go for it. If he could put on an Elvis costume and perform for hundreds of strangers, why couldn't he find the courage to have a conversation with the one person who meant everything to him? Because he was afraid of how that conversation would go. He needed a sign.

He drove home, his thoughts going around in his head. He fed Geralt and gave him a quick hug and kiss. Then he logged onto his computer and loaded the messenger app, ready to run the search he did every day, just in case. He typed GoodGirlKay into the search bar ready to read the words, *We couldn't find what you were looking for, try again?* But instead her profile popped up. His heart thumped with excitement. She was there?

He clicked onto it and it brought up her picture, seeing her face flooded him with so much happiness that he knew he needed to fight for her. He couldn't sit back and do nothing, no matter how scared he was because this would get him nowhere. She wasn't online so he didn't message her, but it was enough that she had unblocked him. That was the sign he'd needed.

The urge to see her was riding him hard, but she wasn't home, and she wasn't at the bar.

"Wait a minute," he murmured, leaping for his phone, fumbling with it and bringing it to his face, checking the day and time. He knew exactly where she was.

With another quick ruffle of Geralt's fur, Ben grabbed his keys and ran out the door. Speeding across one town and driving through another until he pulled up outside that neon sign of hope: *Intrigue*.

He was so proud of her for continuing her lessons, for her courage. Courage that he had needed to find for himself to come after her, to face potential rejection in order to fight for her, for what they had.

And when she stepped out of those doors ten minutes later, he knew it was all worth it.

She stopped short when she saw him, leaning against his car, surprise on her beautiful face. He noticed her peach hair was fading slightly, her natural light brown color fighting its way through. She looked like her old self, OG Kayleigh.

"Need a lift home?" he asked, a slight tremble of fear in his voice.

Kayleigh looked down the street before back to him, and when she nodded, triumph flared through him. He opened the door for her and stepped back, her spiced apple scent teasing him as she got in.

The journey was silent, he didn't say anything and neither did she. He wanted to pull his thoughts together and by the time they arrived at her house, he was ready. He switched off the car and faced her, her blue eyes glimmering with questions.

"I'm sorry. What I did was an incredible violation, not to mention ethically questionable, and hurtful. I was so scared that you would be mad I had come looking for you that I pretended we were strangers when we weren't. We were best friends, on the cusp of becoming something more, not that you knew how much I cared for you. We had a connection unlike any I've ever experienced, the kind you read about, the kind that people write songs about. How could I not follow my heart and find you?"

She sniffled. "It's not like I had never asked you to move here. I just figured that if you ever took me up on that offer, you would tell me who you were."

He shook his head. "I should have been upfront and honest with you about who I was from the start, and I can never apologize enough for not doing that. I didn't mean to trick you or deceive you, that was never my intention. I just wanted my friend. My love. There's no one like you Kayleigh, you thrill me."

She sniffled again and he looked over at her, her eyes pooling with tears. He ached to comfort her, he reached a hand across the space between them, pausing, giving her a chance to pull away before he took her hand in his. Her skin soft like velvet, he brought her hand to his lips.

"Please tell me I haven't ruined the best thing that ever happened to me?" he rasped, his throat thick with emotion. Silence filled the car, loaded with tension and emotion so strong he almost couldn't bear it.

Finally, she spoke. "Why are cats so good at video games?

Relief flooded him and a smile fought at his lips as he pretended to ponder her question. "Because they have nine lives?"

She nodded, her shy smile producing those adorable dimples that he loved and with a groan he kissed her knuckles again, never more grateful in his life to hear one of her jokes. He pulled her onto his lap and cupped her face with both hands, pressing urgent kisses over her lips, cheeks and jaw before she captured his mouth with a slow, sensual tongue-twisting kiss that left him panting and begging for more.

"God, I love you." He pulled back, brushing a lock of hair behind her ear, stroking his thumb over the apple of her cheek.

She nibbled her lip, looking away briefly before she met his gaze again. "I love you, too."

He pushed out a deep breath at her words. He hadn't expected to hear them, but no words had ever sounded sweeter.

"Be my player two?" he whispered.

She smiled and pressed a kiss to his lips. "Absolutely."

Two Months Later...

Kayleigh screamed along with the rest of the crowd at The Rusty Bucket Inn, desperate to get to him, elbowing Ruby out the way and not feeling bad about it one bit. That man on stage was hers and she needed everyone to know it.

He had said to her a couple of weeks ago that he struggled to concentrate when she was in the audience, watching the way her hips swayed. Staring up at him all she could think was, *same.*

One song came to an end, and he winked down at her, his eyes afire with a heat and longing that had her insides quivering before he launched into the next one. He belonged to her, and no one could deny it.

His song was about reflection, and it got her thinking. About the journey that both of them had been on, both trying to grow and become the people they were meant to be. Both worried about what other people thought of them instead of owning it.

Luckily, together they had found the courage to accept themselves and chase their dreams. Ben continued to perform as Elvis, booking various performances throughout the state which sometimes took him away for too long, but she didn't begrudge it, it gave her time to write and time to miss him and to look forward to his return. He was fast on his way to becoming a huge sensation and was exploring how to make this his sole career. Kayleigh figured he was well on his way, he was in high demand after finding a new audience on TikTok and she couldn't be more thrilled for him.

Kayleigh knew it hurt that his father couldn't put his feelings aside and support him. But Matt had reached out and they were slowly working through the repair of their relationship. He had come to visit Ben a couple of weeks ago, the first time since he'd turned up at the bar with his father. Ben said the meeting had been tense but it sounded like it was the beginning of a new relationship, and Matt would be back again next week so see Ben perform.

Kayleigh had started her narrative design and screenwriting course last month at the community college in Palm Valley, not far from Citrus Pines. She was applying for junior roles at a few larger gaming corporations across the state. Most of them offered working from home and she would only occasionally need to travel into an office, but they could make it work. Both her and Ben were following their dreams and supporting each other.

Ben finished his set to thunderous applause and screams from the packed bar. Taylor loved being able to secure performances from him because he brought in crowds from all over. The Ladies' Nights continued to be a success, as had the LGBTQIA nights they had begun hosting. Kayleigh couldn't believe the reception they'd had and was so pleased to see more people finding the love they deserved, just like she had.

His arms banded around her, pulling her tight against him. "You drive me wild," he murmured into her ear, his breath tickling the shell, and goosebumps covered her skin.

"Same," she replied before spinning around in his arms and kissing him. When they broke apart, he asked, "How was *Intrigue?*"

"So good! I can hold myself upside down now."

He grinned down at her, shaking his head. "Incredible! You amaze me."

She pressed a kiss to his lips. "Then hold onto your hat buddy, I've got a surprise for you."

"Oh yeah? I've got something for you too." He waggled his eyebrows, and she rolled her eyes, her smile never leaving her face.

She produced the tickets from her purse and handed them to him.

His eyes flew to hers when he realized what she was showing him. "We're going to Memphis?"

"Uh huh."

"Graceland?"

"Obviously."

"Beale Street?"

"Yes," she laughed. "We can do it all, everything you want to look at and get your fill of all things Elvis."

"God, I love you." He kissed her again, slow and deep. It wasn't the first time he'd said it, it was one of many, but she kept the memory of each one locked away in a little piece of her heart, treasuring every single one.

"I love you, too."

"Now, let me show you something outside," he said with meaning, pulling her down the hallway and out the back of the bar, the cool air tickling her bare legs. He had her up against the side of the building and his hand under her skirt in two seconds flat. When his fingers slipped inside her, she moaned.

"Feels like the first time," he breathed against her lips.

"No fair, Beau, they found our make out spot!" Came a whine from next to them.

Kayleigh squeaked with surprise and Ben moved in front of her, shielding her from view. She peeked over his shoulder and saw Taylor and her boyfriend, Beau, illuminated by the moonlight.

"It's okay sweetheart, we'll find a new one," Beau said, dragging Taylor away.

"Just remember, she loved me first!" Taylor shouted over her shoulder at Ben. Kayleigh's shoulders shook from laughter.

"I don't know what you're finding so funny about this whole thing. You're not the one with a boner in a white satin suit they *definitely* just got an eyeful of," Ben grumbled.

She burst out laughing again before he pinned her to the wall of the bar with his pelvis, lifting her leg to wrap around his hip. "I remember last time you weren't so happy at being discovered out here *in flagrante*."

She rolled her hips against him eager for more pressure. "What can I say, I'm a changed woman."

"You certainly are, you're not really a good girl at all, are you Kayleigh?" His deep timbre shredded her nerves.

She shook her head before slowly sinking to her knees. He grunted as she ran her hand over the aching length of him and his hand tunneled into her hair.

"There's my bad girl..."

The End.

Other Books By Lila Dawes

Citrus Pines Series

Book1: It's Only Love

Book 2: Color of Love

Book 3: Sweet Surrender

Book 4 Love Me Good

Book 5: TBC follow me for updates!

If this is your first trip to Citrus Pines, then I hope you enjoyed it and if you can't get enough then head back to the beginning with Christy & Dean's HEA, It's Only Love.

Acknowledgements

Thank you so much for reading Kayleigh & Ben's novella, I really hoped you enjoy it and please consider leaving a review on Goodreads, Amazon and any socials you have. Reviews really help indie authors and we need all the help we can get from awesome readers like you.

Huge thank you as always to my alpha's; Mimi, Anna P and Anna L – your feedback, love for B & K and support really helped me through the novella writing process which I was unimpressed to find is just as damn tough as a full-length novel. My beta's; Holly June, Michelle, Lou, Ingrid, Julie and Marianne thank you so much for all your feedback and comments, I truly appreciate your input and support.

Massive thank you to my editor for getting this ship shape and for highlighting just how appalling I am with comma's. I'm so glad you loved the word *dickmatized!*

Finally thank you to my ARC readers, seeing your amazing reviews come in gives me such a boost. Imposter syndrome is a needy, aggressive bitch and each lovely review from you helps tell it to shut the hell up xx

About the Author

Lila is a thirtysomething writer living in Derbyshire, England with her *cough* parents *cough*. She loves romance, sharks, cats and has an ~~un~~healthy obsession with Henry Cavill.

Love Me Good is the fourth novel in the Citrus Pines series, head to Amazon to check out the series if you haven't already! Lila is a huge fan of the romance reading and writing community so why not say hello, she can be found on Instagram, Facebook, Pinterest, Tiktok, Goodreads and contacted via her shiny new website www.liladawesauthor.com.

Printed in Dunstable, United Kingdom